GYPSY

Preethi Nair worked as a management consultant and gave it up to follow her dream and complete her first book, *Gypsy Masala*. Having been rejected by a number of publishers, she set up her own publishing company and PR agency to promote the book. Working under the alias of Pru Menon, Preethi managed to get substantial coverage and subsequently signed a three-book deal with HarperCollins. She won the Asian Woman of Achievement award for her endeavours and was also shortlisted as publicist of the year for the PPC awards. Her second novel, *One Hundred Shades of White*, has been bought by the BBC for a television adaptation. Her third book, *Beyond Indigo*, has just been published alongside this revised edition of *Gypsy Masala*.

Preethi now lives in London where she has spent most of her life.

Praise for Preethi Nair:

'A little gem of fiction . . . a mystic and beautifully lyrical book.'   *New Woman*

'This book will have you praying for a delayed train.'
                                                                        Glamour

'A genuinely moving novel.'   *Daily Express*

'She writes evocatively about childhood and there are passages of tight and lyrical immediacy.'   *Guardian*

'A warm-hearted tale of survival.'   *The Bookseller*

PREETHI NAIR

Gypsy Masala

HarperCollins*Publishers*

HarperCollins*Publishers*
77–85 Fulham Palace Road,
Hammersmith, London W6 8JB

www.harpercollins.co.uk

First published by Ninefish 2000
This revised edition published by HarperCollins*Publishers* 2004
1

A catalogue record for this book
is available from the British Library

ISBN 0 00 714347 8

Typeset in Sabon by Palimpsest Book Production Limited,
Polmont, Stirlingshire

Printed and bound in Great Britain by
Clays Ltd, St Ives plc

Dedicated to you the reader, in the hope that you may follow the African dancer.

EVITA

'Go away phantom sore throat, untie the muffler and release me so that I may go forth and conquer all that lies before me.'

I have always been a drama queen. I can remember being about seven, scarf tied around my neck, sitting with my Auntie Sheila and her friends listening to incessant banter and clattering coffee cups. Suddenly, I would bolt forth, untie my scarf and ask Argentina not to cry for me. My aunties would stop their slurping and look at me with bewildered eyes. Twenty years later, Evita plays on and the echo of that child resounds deep within me.

I want to bring back this crazy, impetuous child – just for an instant – so I can jump out of my chair at work and tell my boss what I really think of him. And then, maybe, I will stop making excuses and finally escape the mundane routine of a 9–5 existence.

A lot has happened over the past few weeks, and in order to think about things and to locate the little girl I once was, I have feigned illness – the sore throat to be precise – taking a few days off work only to develop the real thing. Cosily tucked up under my duvet, muffler around my neck, my mind wanders.

When I was about eight and played the Virgin Mary in the nativity, I looked at smiling, innocent little Joseph and questioned why he was wearing a tea towel on his head. Indeed, why was I wearing one on my head? The Angel Gabriel and the three shepherds just yawned and accepted the situation, whilst I further contemplated how I had managed to conceive a baby Jesus who was not of ethnic origin.

I took that plastic baby Jesus in hand and threw him into the audience where my Auntie Sheila was sitting. She shared their stern, dismayed looks. It was then I knew that things were going to be difficult.

Not that things prior to that incident had not been difficult. Having lost my own parents in an accident, a long, dusty road had led me to the doorstep of the Vishavans. I'm not too sure about the details of how I arrived there but it was my Auntie Sheila and my Uncle Bali who brought me up. They were a very practical couple and veering away from the realms of reality into flights of imagination was strictly prohibited. The consequences were dire: at best there would be stern looks of disapproval from my Auntie Sheila, and at worst the fear of further abandonment forever loomed around me.

So, like one of those little messages, I have managed to

make myself fit into a bottle and have bobbed up and down for a long time now on the crest of other people's expectations. Desperately yearning for the bottle to break but not quite sure what I'll do if it does.

Tired of summoning up the courage to try and make my great escape, I closed my eyes on that Sunday evening and fell into a deep sleep. I can't quite recollect the whole dream but I remember fragments of it, such as embarking on a journey and seeing different people with what looked like huge coals inside of them. These coals were lit by their dreams, their hopes and expectations, and their eyes either glowed or were dull and listless. Someone, I think it was a woman, approached me and asked me what my dream was, and just as I was about to answer I was awoken by the very faint sound of a drum. And then, as my eyes half-opened, I caught a glimpse of a little African figure dancing across my room. He jumped out of my bedroom window.

'Come follow me,' he whispered.

Deeply regretting downing half a bottle of brandy the night before to anaesthetise my throat, I dragged myself up, vowing to get a firm grip on reality.

'Come follow me,' I heard the voice whisper again.

I know that this is what I heard clearly, but fearing insanity I quickly turned on the radio and made my way into the shower.

* * *

It was freezing that Monday morning. I was on the Underground going to work, heading towards Baker Street, willing there to be no further delays due to the forecasted snow falling on the tracks. Luckily, because I had left earlier than usual, the carriages were not as jam-packed as they could have been.

To my right, a couple were seated. He, in his mid-thirties, attempted to read the newspaper, and she, clinging on to his arm, evaporated into him. Not far from them was a man with a beard and a huge coffee-coloured mac and opposite me sat a dark-skinned woman dressed in fine magenta, wearing numerous gold bracelets. I thought not only must she be cold but also brave for exposing them like that, but judging from her attire I figured she must have come from afar and not been aware of the concept of muggings, or snow for that matter. She appeared totally misplaced, sitting amongst all the people in their grey suits. Finding her a strange curiosity, I studied her even more closely. Her eyes looked like still puddles; I could see myself in them. No one I'd ever met had eyes like that. She must have come from a faraway island and been a princess or something. The princess, though, had chipped nail-varnish.

As I looked at her nails and contrasted them to her whole demeanour, it reminded me of the fact that perfection does not exist – everyone has something missing. It was probably best to see things as imperfect, to have no expectations so that things could not come crashing down. This is what my Auntie Sheila had endeavoured to teach me. But why was it that I was incapable of doing this? Perhaps because I am a dreamer; I dream of infinite possibilities because there must be more to life than just this.

Passengers got on at Finchley Road and hunted for space in the carriage. As one of the commuters sat on the end of the bearded man's mac he huffed in an irritated manner and then shuffled along his seat and sprawled his news-paper across his lap. He then emitted a defiant 'tut' as the coat-creaser began freely reading his paper. Being on the Underground in some way seemed to incite the most rodent-type behaviour. People become incredibly predatory over their space. Maybe it is because they want to feel safe and secure.

Perhaps there is no real security or safety, just a perceived sense of one. Things happen from out of the blue that you cannot account for, random acts of fate. In my case it was my parents dying, so I think it's pointless trying to control things. This is what I believe deep down inside but this is not how I act; possibly because I don't want to hurt my Auntie Sheila and my Uncle Bali by going against every-thing they have tried to instil in me, or maybe this is just my excuse. So I remain cosseted in the life that they have given me, not venturing out of all that I know, except, that is, in the world of my imagination.

I scrutinised the face of the man who huffed and tutted: he looked unhappy. The crumpled end of a coat is not worth that amount of unhappiness. As I sat watching all the different types of people and imagined what their lives were like, I wondered if they were happy, truly happy, and enjoyed what they did; or did they share the same feelings of frustration as me and just waited for their Christmas bonus and then made a whole load of resolutions in the New Year which they knew they would never keep. My Uncle Bali always told me that life wasn't about being happy, it was about getting a stable routine so that you could be buffered by life's disappointments. Just as I was thinking this, I remembered more of the dream about the coals. I searched people's eyes to see if they had realised their dreams or whether they were riding the same beaten track as I was because they were afraid – afraid to do something bold, something different; afraid of disappointing others.

The lady to my right who formed part of the couple had eyes that were completely glazed over. Somehow she had managed to surrender herself to a pair of black stilettos, she squeezed herself into them so that the fragile heels supported the weight of eighty kilos. What did this tall, mousy-blond gentleman have that made her surrender herself not only to her shoes? This wasn't right either, putting all your hopes and expectations into one person – I had done this too. It had ended disastrously, in fact just last week. I was supposed to be getting married until I caught him with his fingers in the locks of a curly brunette.

'Will you give me a ring then at lunchtime and tell me how we'll arrange it?' stiletto lady asked.

The word 'yes' was followed by the word 'darling'. It sounded as if the passion with which he had first spoken those words had ebbed, leaving the sound of hollow letters that made an empty phrase. Does the passion wane in all relationships after a time?

'Shall we get in some of those dips and some bites?' the stiletto lady said, attempting to resuscitate his words.

Mr Mousy continued to read his *FT*. 'Hmmmm . . .' he mumbled.

'And a bottle of red,' she continued.

'Hmmmmm.'

The art of communication was not one of his stronger points. That was what probably attracted her to him in the first instance, hoping that she could change that. Her friends had probably told her not to settle for less, to leave him, that there were plenty more mousies out there in the big blue sea, but this just strengthened her conviction and made her cling to him tighter. Her coals were probably kept alight by the thought of being with him.

And then amongst the group of random strangers in that tube carriage, there was me. My real name is Molu: Molu Vishavan. I'm twenty-seven years old. I used to be a Cancerian but on arriving at my Auntie Sheila's house she changed my birthday so I am now a Scorpio. I have had two failed serious relationships, one near-miss at marriage, and I still live at home with my adoptive parents, Sheila and Bali, and still sleep with the light on. I have decided to change my name to Evita because I don't want to be me any more; I want to leave the security and the safety of all that I know and embark upon a crazy adventure.

Staring at the reflection as I leaned against the tube window, I looked like anything but an adventurer. My hair was longer than it needed to be and swamped my face, and my eyes did not sparkle. The woman dressed in magenta saw me studying myself and smiled at me. Embarrassed, I looked away, wanting to tell her that it wasn't because I was vain but because I had this dream and I didn't think I was big enough to realise it.

'Follow him,' the woman in magenta whispered.

I looked up in utter amazement.

'Excuse me, what did you just say?'

'You have seen him. Just follow him.'

She then got up. I wanted to tell her not to go, to run behind her, but I was too shocked to say or do anything and then she disappeared.

'Did you hear that, did you hear what that woman just said?' I wanted to shout to the other passengers in the carriage.

But they continued to ride the train, consumed by their own thoughts. Some nodded off into their papers, eyes shut, mouths half-open. Then, by some miraculous force, once they reached their stop they would suddenly awake.

I wanted to close my eyes and wish that the same mysterious force would wake me too. I didn't want to see what other people didn't. I didn't want to do this on my own.

The train arrived at Baker Street.

My job is the most uninspiring, monotonous work in the history of economic periodicals. I work as a researcher for the publishers of one.

What I do most of the day is call up heads of Fortune 500 companies and ask them how they invest their money. This is done by a series of questions on derivatives, swaps and the foreign exchange. It sounds complicated but it's pretty simple really as all the questions are written out on a script which I read through whilst ticking lots of boxes. This is then handed over to Stephen Kolinsky, a nerdy guy with glasses who's our data analyst. And then I go down my contacts list and begin again. I often wonder how on earth I got into it – perhaps it was the wording on the job advertisement – 'working with scripts' – that lured me.

I'd always wanted to be an actress and my Auntie Sheila keeled over when I first told her. Her impressions of what it was to be an actress went something like this: images of an Indian woman with a wet sari clinging to her body in the rain, prancing around like a stunned fairy. In between some kind of sing-song, the protagonist, seeing her lover jumping from behind the trees like a flasher, runs off whimsically, refusing his advances. After a pursuit involving running round and round the same tree, a frenzied disco dance erupts between them. It was that 'filthy' love scene etched in her mind that summed up what an actress was, so, understandably, she was having none of it.

Instead, I tried to get her to take me to the theatre but she couldn't understand why anyone would want to dress up and pretend to be someone else. My Auntie Sheila is firmly grounded in reality and the only flights of fancy she has is going to Tesco's and picking up a deluxe chocolate gateaux, or 'ga-tux' as she pronounces it. So there was no persuading her to send me to stage school. Instead, she sent me to a private school and selected the appropriate course for me to study at university. It sounds weak now to say I just went along and did what she wanted, but I did it to keep the peace: it was a household fraught with tension.

Sometimes at work, to vary my script-reading technique, I read the questions with different accents. The American one seemed to go down quite well, as did the Italian. CEOs weren't so hot on the Nigerian one as it seemed to take me forever to get through: I had to keep repeating things and eventually they lost their patience. But sometimes the heads of these corporations would flirt outrageously with these fictitious characters and I would create whole lives that didn't exist – and that, sadly, is how I got through my days. That, and going to the cinema and theatre at every possible opportunity and envisaging myself on stage.

My boss caught me doing the accent thing last week. He reprimanded me in front of everyone, saying we were not running some sleazy call-service, and asked me to think very carefully about my career. He didn't realise that thinking about my career was what I had been doing ever since I started three years ago. That very same lunchtime I caught my fiancé, Avinash Kavan, with his fingers in the locks of a curly headed brunette. It was time to face facts – hence my hasty retreat into bed and the sore throat that followed.

That Monday morning as I walked into work, I didn't know what to believe. Confused, I sat at my desk and pulled out the script along with the list of contacts to call for the day. A few friends at work asked if I was feeling better. 'Yes, a whole lot better,' I replied, hoping not to give away any signs of mental instability.

What had happened to me? Was it real? I sat staring out of my window.

The office had two large windows. Sitting next to one of them was one of the perks of the job. I had bagsied it when my friend Elaine, who was sitting there previously, plucked up the courage to leave. My colleagues only let me have it because they fell about laughing at the word 'bagsie' – 'bagsie the window' to be precise, said just as her office stationery was being redistributed. However, the windows were kept firmly shut. I had tried to un-jam mine at various times but to no avail. As a result, all the tension collected during the day, and left with the staff at home-time when the doors were opened.

The primary source of this tension emanated from my boss, a bald-headed man who backcombed the four remaining strands of his dyed hair and who strapped himself into some ill-fitting trousers by using a pair of antiquated braces. He would pounce from behind us when we were on the telephone and do a post-mortem on the things we got wrong, never praising us for the things we got right. After I had put the telephone down last week he had begun swearing at me for pretending to be Onsawawa Bonumboto.

'Feeling yourself again?' he sneered when he saw me back at work.

'Yes thank you. Everything is under control,' I replied politely.

'Back to it, then.'

I opened the script, switched on my computer and began gazing at my screensaver.

What if the coal thing was true; what if people were ignited and called to adventure by listening to their dreams? What did a burning flame inside you feel like? Did it get rid of all the doubts, the fears? Who was this little man who jumped out of my bedroom window? Why did the lady in magenta say she saw him? Did she mean him? What if I was going crazy? Was this covered under my medical protection plan?

The sounds of the fax machines and telephones seemed to get fainter and fainter. One resounding thought was beating like a drum in my head. Who was he? The sound of the drum grew louder and louder. I could no longer control it. The thought bounced out of my head and manifested itself in the shape of a dancer. It was the same African dancer from this morning. He ran along my keyboard and across the screen, unravelling himself before me.

A slight tremor of a rhythm took a hold of my fingers and I began to type out my resignation letter. It was almost as if my fingers worked automatically, requiring no thought from me. After I'd typed it, I reached for an envelope, stuffed the letter inside and walked over to my boss's desk. The dancer followed beside me.

The tension which had knotted in my throat during the last three years diffused into the air as the letter landed on his desk. An enormous smile spread across my face. My boss stared at me; I looked at the dancer next to me but he was heading off towards my closed window.

'No, don't go,' I wanted to scream.

But it was too late; he had somehow managed to jump out.

I grabbed my coat and ran out to find him but he had gone.

Frantically running up and down Marylebone High Street, I searched for him. He was nowhere to be found. It was insane; I'd left my job on the basis of a figment of my imagination. I sat in a doorway and began to cry. What was I thinking of? What was happening to me? As I held my head in my hands, I felt someone touch my shoulder. I saw sandals and toes with pink chipped nail-varnish. I did not dare look up.

'Follow the African dancer, my child; take your heart in your hands and follow him. As you walk, tread firmly on fear, clear the path and let the African dancer dance; dance his way into reality.'

When I managed to glance up, she had disappeared.

Once the decision had been taken to follow the African dancer, the laws of nature somehow conspired and I found myself riding on the crest of a tidal wave that propelled me to a faraway land.

It was a similar sort of journey to the one that I had made as a small child, in the sense that I don't quite remember the specifics of how I got there. All I know was that one moment I was living happily with my grandmother on her farm in rural India, playing with calves, chickens and goats. Then, suddenly, on a flip of a coin, I had to exchange all that for a battered merry-go-round, swings and slides, and this couple called the Vishavans whom I had never met before.

Twenty-two years later it was a similar scenario: one moment I was crying on the pavement in Marylebone High Street and the next I was on a beach, far off the beaten track.

* * *

I woke up confused and dazed, trying to find my bearings. The sun dazzled my eyes, my head was throbbing and my hair was covered in sand. As I hauled myself up, an old man approached me.

'Ma'am, a watch for your beautiful wrist, or perhaps a necklace?'

I looked towards my wrist and found I was still wearing my suit. I shook my head, and when I finally managed to speak I asked if he knew where I was.

'It's not so important to know this now – just know your call for adventure was heard.'

'What do you mean?'

'It was relentless. Every day, all we heard was, "Please get me out of here. I don't know how, but please do it." You never stopped and now you have taken a leap of faith and come here of your own accord.'

'But where am I? What's going on?'

'You are wherever you want to be.'

Surely half a bottle of brandy could not have this effect a day later. I looked around and panicked at the unfamiliar surroundings. There was no one on that empty beach, no big umbrellas, no sun-beds, nothing except two sets of footprints that belonged to the old man and me. Trying to gain some sense of perspective, I turned around and my breath was almost taken away. There behind me, as far as the eye could see, was lush green foliage and the peak of a glorious purple mountain.

'It's beautiful, truly beautiful, but I . . .'

'Just breathe, breathe very deeply.' The old man inhaled slowly through his nose.

And so I did, trying to calm myself, allowing my breath to flow in unison with the waves and allowing the sea air to empty my head of all thoughts.

'Good. Do you feel better now?'

I nodded. 'Please can you help me? I don't know how I came to be here; I came in search of an African dancer.'

'I know,' he replied. 'Many come in search of him.'

'So he's real and you know what I'm talking about.'

The old man laughed. 'Suspend your disbelief, Evita.'

How did he know that I had decided to call myself Evita?

'How do you know that I call myself Evita?'

'I know many things about you – I know that in the mornings you like two sugars in your coffee, that you stir the spoon endlessly, dreaming about ways of escaping the confines of your reality.'

I looked at him with disbelief.

He continued, 'I know that at the end of the day you write down three things that you are grateful for, and you do this to remind yourself how lucky you are – even on the days you don't feel lucky.'

And as he spoke, giving me the intimate details about myself that nobody could have known about, a horn sounded, piercing the calmness with its odd tune. An engine roared and a taxi pulled up beside us.

'Good,' the old man said, 'José is here. He will look after you from here on – anything you need, you ask him.'

'You can't leave me. I have so many questions for you.'

'Save them. Be patient, Evita. Time is your friend and you will find the answers to all of your questions. Trust in the adventure.'

With that, he turned and walked in the opposite direction.

'Please don't leave me,' I shouted.

He continued walking.

A thin man got out of the taxi and approached me. He was wearing a white shirt which was obviously too tight for him; the buttons looked constipated and miserable and the trousers were supposed to match but made him look like a straw. A bushy moustache rested upon his lip and looked as if it had been stuck on.

'Allow me to present myself, Miss Evita – my name is José Del Rey, King of the Taxi Drivers,' he said proudly. 'I am your host and at your complete disposal.'

This was getting stranger but I felt reassured because his taxi reminded me of my grandfather's old car and also because there was a picture of Jesus and a wooden cruci-fix dangling from the rear-view mirror. As I climbed in the back, I noticed that the seats were done up in what appeared to be leopard-skin upholstery.

'Good fashion, no?' José Del Rey asked as he spotted me eyeing it.

'Doesn't it get a bit hot and sweaty?'

'I have air-conditioning for you,' he replied. At which point he blasted it on full fan.

'You couldn't turn it down just a bit? It's only because I suffer from sore throats.'

'Here you won't suffer from anything. The air will cure everything. Where you want to go?' he asked.

'Up into the mountain, I think.'

'This is a good idea, this is where I was going to take you. You're here for nine days I'm told.'

Was I? Was it some package tour?

'It is enough to experience it all,' he added.

For the first time, I began to feel slightly excited. It didn't matter how I had got there. The fact was I was there, and would endeavour to make the most of it.

The significance of the crucifix came to light as José Del Rey attacked the emerging hairpin bends with the vigour and ferocity that belonged only to someone who did not fear death. The crucifix swayed from side to side as he accelerated round the corners.

'You all right back there, Miss Evita?' he asked.

'Clutch control,' I shouted.

'What?'

'You couldn't slow down just a bit? I don't think I am in any hurry.'

20

He looked at me through the rear-view mirror and patted his moustache. 'You are safe with me, miss. This is why they call me King of the Taxi Drivers. I know these roads like I know my own mother.'

Perhaps it was a phrase that didn't translate well into English. I lingered on the thought of how well he could know his own mother. If she was anything like my Auntie Sheila, who had no-entry signs bobbing up all over the place, then we were in grave danger.

José Del Rey appeared to slow down as we got higher into the mountain. The air felt lighter, the greenery was dense; it was cooler and fresher. As I rolled down the window I could hear a faint drumbeat. I watched women with huge urns move as if they carried the rhythm within them, and children were dancing barefoot on the road. José Del Rey sounded his horn as we passed them, at which point they began running after us.

As we approached a plateau, the drumbeats grew louder and louder.

'Two minutes,' José Del Rey indicated with his fingers. There were houses painted in pastel colours dotted about. I could see a village square – it wasn't a defined square with a focal point such as a church surrounded with benches or anything like that, just a simple open space where people congregated.

Both young and old were listening to the musicians who had brought out their drums and most people were dancing to the rhythm. As the taxi pulled up, a few people stared and smiled – welcoming smiles. Some of the boys who had followed us asked José if they could sit in his taxi. He shook his head defiantly.

I got out of the car feeling very self-conscious in my suit.

'My wife is somewhere here, but if you want to go to the house first, I take you there.'

'Is that where I'm staying?'

'Yes, in our humble abode. Unless you want me to take you somewhere else?'

'No, thank you. I'm very grateful.'

He patted his moustache and held out his elbow as a gesture for me to take it.

I marvelled at the people dancing so freely. They carried a different rhythm in them, one that was so passionate and carefree. It could not have been more different to the sounds of North London – the drone of the traffic; people locked away in their houses.

José introduced me to his wife, Delores, who was holding her son's hand. She looked about the same age as I was and her son José could not have been more than seven or eight.

'Welcome,' Delores said. 'José, welcome our guest.'

The little boy pulled a face and I pulled one back at which point he laughed.

'You must be tired. Come, have something to eat.'

As I sat down in the square, plates of food were thrust forward from nowhere, and because I was so hungry I did not sit and savour the flavours, colours and aromas, eating so fast, like I had never been fed.

The night owl called bedtime like last orders, but people took no notice of the fact that night beckoned. Fires were built in a bid to keep it at bay. People stopped dancing and sat in a circle to talk and eat.

There on the mountain, mouths filled with food and conversation. Hot chillies gave fire to the blood and propelled words out with vivacity. Elders told stories whilst youngsters sat in their laps. It took me back to my early childhood when my grandfather would tell me stories in an attempt to put me to sleep.

Little José's grandfather was recounting the tale about how the rains came. José went to sit next to him.

'So the old lady, Emelda, who was against the union, shouted, "If you marry my son" (for he was her only son), "nobody here will ever dance."'

Although it appeared as if the little boy had heard the story a thousand times, he sat even closer to his grandfather and urged him to continue.

'So the spell was cast as the couple married. The old woman did not realise that she was part of the land that grew arid. She became cynical and twisted until death took her. There in the skies, she wandered aimlessly, lost because there was no one to love her or to shout up silent prayers that they missed her. The burden showed markedly in her posture, her stomach folded and her footsteps became heavy. Totally alone, she could bear it no longer and she cried and cried, begging forgiveness as she did so. The tears, sour at first, lost their bitterness as they touched the ground, bringing new life to all. Those tears were the rain that provided fertile lands on which the people celebrated and danced. From that, the rain came every year.'

Little José battled unsuccessfully with nightfall. He fell asleep on his grandfather's lap, and I, also exhausted, took a stick and under the night stars wrote the words 'thank you' into the ground. I was truly thankful to be here, wherever here was, feeling for the first time in a long time completely free and myself amongst the company of generous strangers who did not make me miss home, understanding that home could be anywhere you wanted it to be.

The next morning Delores stormed out of the house. She was going to find her husband, José Del Rey, King of the Taxi Drivers. When she eventually tracked him down, she would rip off his moustache, the fake symbol of his manhood, and then toss it into the river. Mother Earth would surely know it was his and would then castigate him in some way for having polluted her in such a distasteful manner.

It was alleged late last night that José Del Rey had been

giving lifts freely to women of a more rounded figure. Delores slept on what she had heard, trying not to give it importance. During the course of the night, the anger simmered inside her until she could take it no more.

They had been married ten years. José Del Rey had been sent to her in his crisp white shirt just eight days before she was due to marry someone else. He came from nowhere and she knew instinctively that he was the one she wanted to spend the rest of her life with.

I've always believed this kind of scenario to be made up, having talked to my Auntie Sheila and Uncle Bali about it and having never really experienced it myself. But I believed Delores Del Rey when she told me that it was possible to love someone in the moment of meeting them.

Taken aback by his charm, his vision and his passion, Delores left her fiancé in a storm of scandal which she never quite managed to live down. At times like this, she regretted having made such a decision. Life was not easy with José Del Rey, but it was different. And despite the drama, anyone could see that they loved each other, from the glances they shared to the way he called her name and touched her fingertips when he thought no one was looking.

Delores returned later that morning with a look of relief. Reports that afternoon suggested that José Del Rey's moustache had been seen floating along the river, face down.

It was really quite unfortunate that Encarna had not heard

the news. Encarna was one of those women with a more rounded body who had accepted a free ride or two from the King of the Taxi Drivers; in fact, rumour had it that she was the one who had enticed him into giving her rides.

Whilst Encarna was collecting water from the river, the moustache had somehow managed to crawl its way into her urn. She placed the urn into her stone-cladded bathroom, undressed and then proceeded to soap herself. Whilst rinsing away the soap with the water from the urn, at the most inappropriate moment the moustache pounced out at her. She hollered in fright at the thought of the rat-infested waters. In so doing, she slipped and crashed to the ground.

That afternoon's event resulted in a broken ankle. The moustache was laid to rest. Encarna sat by the river that whole evening, bathing her leg in the hope that the magical waters would restore it to its former beauty.

As the main aorta, the River Aynia ran from the top of the mountain into the sea. There were several tributaries, some of which had dried up. Aynia brought life to people, she ran through them; and in return, people brought life to her. Generations bathed, drank, washed their clothes and urinated in the same well. Then, as a customary parting gift, their ashes were sprinkled into her.

I was informed by Delores Del Rey that if I followed Aynia for exactly four kilometres I would come to an enormous bougainvillea tree, and on turning left and following this path it would lead me to the Gypsy. Delores said the Gypsy could answer all my questions for she knew everything. She could tell what the significance of the left eye twitching frantically was; she could cure ailments and see the past, present and future.

Delores asked me to make my way to the Gypsy's cabin before José got back from his call-out or he would insist on taking me there, which was pointless because the walk down was equally important as it would give me the clarity to formulate the right questions.

'Remember, Evita, it's not necessarily the answers that are the most important – it's the questions,' she said as I left.

After walking steadily down the mountain, following the path alongside the river, I heard the horn of José's taxi making its way up and dived behind some bushes in case he caught a glimpse of me. After the car roared past me I continued walking and finally came across the tree. It had a magenta blossom and a truly regal presence. Bearing left, I found the wooden cabin and, nervously, I knocked faintly on the door and entered.

Inside, the cabin appeared much bigger than on the outside and resembled a doctor's surgery. There was a waiting room holding an array of people with a multitude of problems – broken bones, twitching eyes, burning ears, and also problems that were not visible to the eye. As the morning came and went, the waiting room emptied.

Encarna was the last one before me to see the Gypsy. I glanced at her leg propped up against the chair.

'Slight misfortune,' she gestured.

'Next,' someone shouted from behind the door.

Encarna hobbled to the consultation room and came out walking perfectly ten minutes later.

'It was not what everyone was thinking,' she said, looking at me. 'There was a therrible, therrible mistake and the Gypsy understood this.' Feeling incredibly anxious and not finding it to be the appropriate time to delve further into the 'therrible mistake' as I would have wanted to, I nodded.

'She's waiting for you,' Encarna shouted as she left.

'Welcome, Evita,' the Gypsy said, turning around to greet me.

I gasped, completely taken aback.

'I've been expecting you. In fact, I thought you'd come sooner,' she said, coming towards me.

'It's . . . it's you,' I mumbled incredulously. It was the woman dressed in magenta with chipped nail-varnish. I went over to touch her to see if she was real. Her hands were soft and elasticy like my grandmother's. I gripped them tightly.

'Would you like some coffee? Two sugars, endlessly stirred?' She smiled.

All the questions that I had silently formulated with

poised composure on my way down were forgotten and something completely different came blurting out. 'How did I get here? Where am I? What's happening to me?'

'One at a time, my dear. This is the land of possibility where intentions are set and dreams manifest into reality,' she replied, putting her hand over mine.

'Where's that then?'

She laughed. 'You know the answer to that.'

'So how did I get here?'

'By leaving all that you know to be true behind – the safety of your home, your family, your routine – you took a leap of faith.'

'It was only because I knew I saw him. I've never seen something like that with such clarity. I've come in search of him you know.'

'I know,' she replied.

'Do you know where he is and how I can find him?'

'He's not as far as people think but few really find him. Some make it their life's work, some come so close but then for reasons that appear mysterious only to others decide to turn back. There are even many who know his exact whereabouts but decide to leave him be, because they know that life can never be the same once they are touched by him. You do know that, don't you? When you follow your dream, your fears will follow you.'

Life would never be the same after this whole episode, regardless. My fears were the least I had to worry about.

'Is he near here somewhere? Am I on the right track?'

'Have patience and all will be revealed to you when you are ready. Focus hard on your intention and then let go. If you do this, he will surrender himself effortlessly.'

'That's all?'

'Just one more thing. Do not stand in your own way by having a fixed set of outcomes, for there is beauty in the adventure of not knowing – of not being certain.' With both hands, the Gypsy clasped my hand so tightly that I wanted to cry. I knew that grip well; my grandmother had done that same thing to me before she sent me off, and I never saw her again.

At that moment I was desperately trying to think of the last thing my grandmother said to me. Many times I have tried to remember.

'When you are unsure of what to do, just be still and listen in here,' the Gypsy whispered, tapping against her chest.

Tears rolled down my face.

'And if you are still unable to hear, just breathe.'

As I walked back to the village I focussed hard on my intention to see the African dancer in whatever shape or form he decided to present himself, and then I attempted to let go by surrendering my desire, thinking that if it didn't work out, another fate, perhaps a better one, would be presented to me.

The boys were all playing in the square as I made my way to the Del Reys' house. A little figure was puffing his way towards them in an attempt to be fully incorporated into the action, if not to become the centre of it. It was little José. The schoolmaster had kept him behind at school for his impertinence.

'Will José be late again in the morning?' inquired the maths teacher.

'Will the maths teacher draw water from the well for his mother every morning?' retorted little José.

It was something I would have said as a child, not fearing the consequences, but as I grew older I understood the complex web of emotions that makes us a prisoner of our own fear.

Little José ran towards the boys, unable to contain the many rumours he had heard that afternoon. There existed something called a Super Information Highway. Yes, that was right, it was called something like that. It was also suggested that the Gypsy was in possession of a modem.

'A modem,' gasped all the boys.

'That was what gave the Gypsy her powers,' continued little José proudly.

He revelled in this piece of information that made the older boys gather around him. Making up whatever he could, he had them all in the palm of his little hand.

It was getting late and Delores left the house to call her son. I watched the look of a mother's angst as she went to go and get him; it was only then I understood the significance of that same face my Auntie Sheila had had when she came to get me.

Little José was also blissfully unaware. He had aspirations ten times higher than himself. They made him grow. All four foot of him just believed. Living in the land of tooth fairies, pixies and magic Kings was effortless. Delores, his mother, was afraid. In just a few years her warrior would be entering adolescence. The world inhabited by eight billion would soon become a battlefield for just one. All alone he would have to confront the battles between dreams and practicalities; the possible and the impossible; the mundane and the extraordinary; the insignificance of the individual placed amongst the significance of the masses. The list went on – and of course, the final conflict, never quite resolved, would be carried through into adulthood. If only I had understood this sooner then things might have turned out differently.

Delores wished that her son would come out unscathed. She hoped that he would retain his vision, his humility and compassion, and would emerge a proud but not arrogant man with the humour and the smile that would continue to melt a thousand hearts, and that the right heart would find him.

But deep down she feared adolescence would take her

little boy. Things that she had said or hadn't said; things that she had done or hadn't done. Blaming the inadequacies of his mother would be a way of comprehending the imperfections of adulthood. But Delores continued to hope. The anxiety left her as she laughed at the thoughts that entered and played inside a mother's head.

She took her little boy's hand. Embarrassed that his friends could have witnessed such an act, he let go and walked behind her.

Staying with the Del Reys gave me an insight into the ups and downs of a truly passionate relationship. Since the Encarna incident, José Del Rey knew that he was skating on thin ice. He put a cigarette to his mouth and was about to light it when Delores pulled it out and trod on it. There was no moustache to hide behind and the frustration was evident. My Uncle Bali would probably not have even dared to light up a cigarette in front of my Auntie Sheila in the first place. Not wanting to aggravate her in any way, he skirted around her, making his presence barely felt.

Days passed, and as I really got to know the Del Reys all thoughts of finding the African dancer seemed secondary. If I returned home with just the experience of being with them, it would be enough. However, as I woke up one morning my instinct was telling me to climb to the top of the mountain and complete my journey.

José Del Rey argued with me, saying he wanted to accompany me, and added that very few who didn't know the terrain made it safely to the top. Having been cushioned and cosseted for most of my life, I knew it was a journey I had to make on my own. Knowing all the consequences of making this trip alone, I set off early, laden with all the necessities José had put together for me. I did not even bother to ask where he had found a miner's helmet complete with built-in light, but he smiled as he put it on my head and patted it.

It was a long, hard walk as the track was undefined. My little toes rubbed against the sides of the boots; pain invaded my feet and exhaustion saturated my body as the pack felt heavier and heavier. The trees grew even denser and brambles cut my hands. As night began to fall my heart leaped with the slightest noise and I feared what bugs would be landing on me. When I felt I couldn't go on and wanted to turn back, I stood still and just breathed and breathed. As I did this, I knew it was up to me to complete what I had begun, and in order to distract my mind I began formulating various questions.

It began to rain. The ground turned slippery, making me feel even more unsure as to whether this was what I was supposed to be doing. But I imagined reaching the top and focussed on my questions as, wearily, I carried on. It was pitch black and freezing when I finally reached the summit. Exhausted, too tired to be frightened by the dark and all the unfamiliar sounds, I stumbled to the ground. With the helmet's light still on, I fell asleep.

When I awoke, the sun shone brightly, turning the mountain-top into a shimmering gold. It was the most breathtaking view that I think I will ever see in my life; an expansive blue sea surrounded by dense green forests with the beginning of the River Aynia glistening against the sun. My body ached all over and I lay there with the sun beaming against my face. After a while I got up, and waited and waited, not quite sure who or what I was waiting for but knowing that I could not leave. And as I closed my eyes, half-dazed, I saw some of the things that I had chosen to forget in my life: the death of my parents, my Uncle Bali taking me from my grandmother, the journey to my Auntie Sheila's house. I understood how everything pieced together and had led to this moment – sitting there, alone on the mountain-top.

As these images passed in front of me, I let them go one by one. I sat with my head resting between my knees and I just cried and cried, a limitless fountain of tears, and then I felt a deep sense of release.

Later that evening, when the mountain-top drew breath, birds and other little animals joined me. They brought with them their anticipation and leaned forward in the hope that they could release it into the air and that life would take care of the details, throwing up some crazy concoction.

The light was dim; my own light was turned off. The moon focussed on the blackened stage. And then he appeared from nowhere – the image of perfection, slender and masculine. The naked torso leaned backwards as his feet took him forward. Then his feet began to tap, slowly, monotonously, to the tempo of everyday life: the commute to work; the nine o'clock start; the commute home. The tapping grew heavier and louder, waking his arms from their deep sleep. In one brusque moment his hands invited the audience to listen, listen to life.

Then, in one almighty move, life exploded and the African dancer danced in front of me. A torrential rain swept across us. The rain fell so hard, washing away all the fears and the doubts as he danced and danced. And at some point late into the night, the dancing stopped and his spirit dissolved slowly into me.

I had found him – anything was possible.

It was freezing cold when the plane arrived at Heathrow airport. Even more so because of having to leave the warmth of that place and the people. As I got off the plane and into the arrivals lounge I noticed that everybody was looking at me. Perhaps I had been beautified by my new aura with the belief that anything was now possible and my look of exhilaration would be attracting only positive things. I was met at the airport by a bag lady who pointed out that the wheels on my suitcase could do with an oiling. 'Too noisy,' she said as she wiped her nose.

I asked her if she knew where the taxis departed from. The bag lady smiled and said she would take me to the stand. She was petite with scraggly grey hair which was housed in a dark brown hat that looked like a tea cosy. She wore a green coat and boots that were two sizes larger than her feet and so as she moved forward her feet tried to make up the gap between the end of her toes and her shoes.

What empty, broken dreams did she carry in those bottles that clinked in her bag? We walked into the lift and she pressed the basement button. Panic filled me as I knew that there was nothing in the basement and I remembered a conversation I had had about bag ladies. Navi, my best friend, had told me to beware of the bag lady. She had heard many a story of men posing as bag ladies only to reveal themselves as knife-wielding maniacs.

We were in the basement and no black cabs were in sight. I could foresee the headlines plastered all over the Heathrow terminal car parks: 'BASEMENT MURDER. DID YOU SEE THIS GIRL OR WOMAN?'

'I just wanted to introduce you to some friends,' said the bag lady.

Friends? I didn't want to meet her friends, I just wanted to find a cab and face my Auntie Sheila.

Somewhere behind the huge metal bins, the happy gang sat, swaying their bottles and singing. I sighed with relief, thinking that they were totally inebriated and could not even pick up a Stanley knife.

'This is Evita,' shouted the bag lady.

How did she know that?

'Evita,' they sang together.

Their group was called 'Resignation'. They were resigned to their fate as bag people; that life had dealt them a cruel set of cards. Life's pathetic failures, bundled up in the basement, out of sight. I turned to walk away from them.

'We heard you've seen him. We've seen him too you know,' said a dead-beat version of Father Christmas.

I stopped in my tracks.

'And we weren't hallucinating,' he added.

Is this what seeing the African dancer led to? A life of picking up passengers from Heathrow airport in a half-intoxicated state? Is this what the Gypsy meant when she said to follow a dream is to follow your fears?

The man read the horror in my face and laughed. 'To achieve, Evita, is to be happy, to stay happy and to make others happy.'

Yes, but happiness for me wasn't sitting in a basement, singing with the happy gang. I wanted more. 'Although the cards have already been dealt,' he continued, 'people have a choice in the hand they play. It is all a matter of choices – make your choices with a full heart and an open mind and you will never go wrong.'

Right. So was this not going wrong?

Then the bag lady went into a monologue as if she were on Broadway. 'Change your perceptions. Do this, and then you'll change your reality. You've got your reality, I've got my reality. Who's got objective reality? The lives of others are different from the perspective you have of them. See the whole picture. Take Mal here, a Forex trader. Pressure, recession, depression, gambled it all away, but he's better than he's ever been. The Ace of Spades – found his pack,' she said slapping him on his back. 'When you reach your height you have to make sure you've got some place else to go, move sideways and take things as they come. We've still got our limos,' she said, looking over at the trolleys filled with plastic bags.

'What happens to me now?' I asked her.

'Whatever you want to happen,' she replied. 'When you break it to your family, be gentle with them,' she added. 'All they have ever wanted for you is the best.'

'I have come to realise this,' I replied. And this was the saddest part of it; that it had taken me so long to understand this.

The happy gang no longer appeared to me as bag people but as a chorus of voices that would do battle with the preconceived ideas that continued to invade my head. I was escorted to the taxi stand to continue the rest of my journey.

* * *

The taxi driver lacked the passion of José Del Rey. He stopped diligently at each set of traffic lights. Waiting for the amber light to flash, he would slowly pull away. Every time he stopped, my stomach churned. This was the part I was dreading: returning home and facing the 'Mob' – the extended family of aunties. The problem was the 'best' that they wanted for me wasn't what I had wanted. As we drew closer to the house, all that had happened on that mountain seemed a distant memory.

I recollected leaving a message hastily on my Auntie Sasha's answer-machine saying that I was going away for a few days and needed time to think. I asked her to inform my Auntie Sheila as I didn't have the courage to do it myself. Asking my Auntie Sheila not to worry about me was like asking the Pope not to be Catholic and she would have somehow managed to persuade me not to go, to come straight back home, for that was the power she had: she could persuade anyone to do anything. Anyone except Sasha, her sister, who invented her own rules away from those of the Mob. She was somehow able to do this whilst pretending to participate wholeheartedly in their antics.

As the cab got closer to our street, my heart began thumping. 'Breathe,' I kept telling myself, 'it will be all right.' But I knew it wouldn't. How could I tell her what I had done; what I was planning to do – that I had no job to go to, that I was going to move out and be an actress? I thought about what the bag lady had told me, to see things from different perspectives, but the facts were clear. My Auntie Sheila would be truly mortified. And then there was the rest of the 'Mob' that she would have to break the news to. They had already been dealt a heavy blow six months earlier when Navi (Auntie Asha's daughter) decided to go travelling for a year. Secret talks were conferred in a bid to dissuade her, a deposit for her own flat was even offered, but to no avail. Navi went. What I was now going to do, especially after my broken engagement, would most probably lead to Auntie Sheila's downfall. Auntie Meena had her eye on the top job and was waiting for an opportunity to step in and take over.

Auntie Sheila was head of the Mob. She drove around in a tinted black BMW with a personalised number-plate that read SHEILA 1. My Uncle Bali had bought this car for her for their thirtieth wedding anniversary last month and the comment she muttered under her breath was 'Sheila didn't win anything.' My uncle had very selective hearing and so he didn't hear this and continued to undo the big pink bow he had put on it as he handed Sheila the keys. Shortly after, Auntie Meena pulled up in our driveway with a new silver Saab convertible – there was no way she could be outdone – and the outside of our house would have looked like a showroom had it not been for my Auntie Sasha's clapped-out Mini Metro, which

Sheila insisted she park on the road, although Sasha didn't.

The founders of the Mob, or those who had any standing, were my aunties Sheila, Sasha, Meena and Asha. In actual fact, none of them were really my aunties. Not by blood, anyway. Out of respect, anyone who looked as if they could be a grown-up (identified from one of a tender age by having a moustache – male or female) had the title of Auntie or Uncle thrust upon them whether they liked it or not.

As I have said before, Auntie Sheila was much more than an Auntie. She became my mother and the emotion that I felt towards her depended upon the state of our relationship at any particular time. Sasha was really her sister and Meena and Asha were friends from twenty years ago. As I understand it, the dynamics of the group had changed considerably as the years passed and those who were on the periphery came and went. The real group dynamics rested with Sheila and Meena who vied with one another in competition. If Sheila had bought a marrow, Meena had a bigger one; if she had her kitchen fitted with the latest appliances, Meena had better ones. Meena was just waiting for her to lose control.

Having said this, despite the political infighting, the Mob remained as one unit. They had strange rituals such as walking out in the sunshine with black umbrellas, holding masonic-like meetings on the fourteenth day of every month where they discussed issues of concern. Whatever rifts they had, they would be healed with a round of somosas, bhajis and a cup of hot tea. It has been like this ever since I can remember, and though these acts of friendship appeared inoffensive, their power was not to be underestimated for the Mob were capable of annihilating a whole population by the mere wagging of their tongues. Nobody would be saved: those with wider hips, darker complexions, gapped teeth, shorties; the list was interminable.

Their respective husbands would attempt to buffer the onslaught by coming to the victims' defence. The weaker ones would be caught up in the crossfire and then would be systematically gunned down. Uncle Bali, Auntie Sheila's husband, was always the first casualty. He never wanted a bad word said against anyone as he said people had their reasons for doing what they did; and then BANG, a sniper comment such as 'You'll always find some excuse,' would be fired in his direction.

How did that come to pass? Looking at the Mob's black and white wedding photos they looked like fragile porcelain dolls, bemused by the sudden transition from teenager to adulthood bestowed upon them by their fathers through matrimony. They were barely capable of keeping the cup and saucer together when meeting their betrothed. My Auntie Sheila's own photo was so moving: she had tears in her eyes and she looked so vulnerable. Where did time take these women? How did they end up so hardened?

The group in her wedding photo looked as if they had escaped from a fancy dress party. There was a man in a soldier's uniform who I was told was Auntie Sheila's father; a nun; a bearded man wearing strange clothes; and my Auntie Sasha in her school uniform. With her comments, Auntie Sheila systematically gunned down every member of the wedding party except the nun, who she said was very kind and gentle. Even Auntie Sasha did not escape a scathing remark. This is what scared me, I suppose: the way she could just coldly cut people off if she disapproved of them. I mean, she did this to her own father without a second thought, not even attending his funeral. My Auntie Sasha sat giving her the details of it all and she appeared completely disinterested.

My Auntie Sasha also annoyed Sheila, for she was vibrant, loud and enthusiastic and just the complete opposite from the silent, composed type that Auntie Sheila was. As a child, I loved playing with my Auntie Sasha as she understood my world of the imagination, being incredibly childlike herself. She understood why people would want to dress up and pretend to be someone else and would take me to see pantomimes and films, but asked me to tell Sheila that we had gone to the park and played in the fresh air instead. It would eventually all come out, though, as Auntie Sasha was not very good at keeping secrets, and then all hell would break loose as my Auntie Sheila was very big on people not telling her lies. But it was Sasha's nature to be mischievous. Once, she accidentally broke one of Sheila's Wedgwood plates and stuffed the two broken bits under the sofa. After promising on my Sindy that it hadn't been me, my Uncle Bali took the blame for it – as he did for many things.

I thought about asking the taxi driver to do a detour to the hospital where Uncle Bali worked so I could talk to him first and we could break the news to Auntie Sheila together, but then I thought better of this as she would probably say it was all his fault. This is what happened when things got too tough for her; she would say that he had left her alone to cope. Which was partly true because of the nature of my Uncle Bali's work commitments, and in fairness to him, like a referee he did occasionally interject with his whistle, but unfortunately Auntie Sheila did not take much notice of this.

As the cab pulled into our street, I imagined my announcement and the look of shock and disbelief.

'An actress?' she would say, keeling over.

My other uncles would not say anything; they rarely said anything except Uncle Govinder, Auntie Meena's husband, who always said that I spoke with a posh accent and had lost all sense of my roots and was now completely English. He would look proudly at his children, Pratesh and Dipshit, the dynamic duo, packaged to us in traditional Indian clothes, who spoke in his presence in a completely Indian accent. Then with their friends they reverted to chameleon mode, really going hard on the 'innit's to make up for the lost language time with their parents.

'Speak like that in English accent only, will bring home white boyfriend, you see,' he announced to the waiting congregation who looked horrified. So, due to his constant criticism, I spoke even posher and would make fun of him.

He said the word yellow as 'ello' and one day I made him say the word yellow three times and then completed the phrase by saying 'what's going on 'ere then?' I don't know why this cheap attempt at being funny made me laugh so much, but he didn't get it.

'Dad, she's taking the piss,' Dipshit said, letting his guard down and his accent slip.

'Piss?' Uncle Govinder repeated.

'Urine,' Dipshit reverted with a strong Indian accent.

He appeared to be slightly confused and said 'No urine taken here.' And then continued sipping his Jack Daniel's.

I never understood why we had to spend so much time with that crazy family, but you name it, every weekend we were there or they came to our house. Thank God for Navi and her brother Jay, because without them life with the dynamic duo would have been unbearable.

Jay and I had some tricky moments. In fact, he was my first boyfriend. As soon as I played with him I knew that I was destined to marry him. I made sure that he understood that I was not some fly-by-night, illicit affair by joining his action man and a shabby-looking doll from the market (who I passed off as a Sindy) in matrimony.

Our relationship was serious: we would hold hands, exchange flirtatious kisses and even share the same straw for our cola. The pressure, I think, just got too much for him and the relationship came to an abrupt end after a heated argument when he broke the legs of my Sindy and rode off on his chopper bike.

I can't even remember what it was over; maybe a misplaced marble, a *Beano*, or perhaps he found out that whilst I was 'banker' at Monopoly, when times were hard I 'borrowed' from my bank. Whatever it was, my Sindy's legs were never the same again and you can't enter Sindy into beauty competitions with the rest of your friends' dolls when her legs keep dropping off even though you know she's not going to win because she's fifty times bigger than everyone else's. It was slightly awkward between us for a time but out of the necessity of not being lumbered with Dipshit and Pratesh, I made an effort with him.

It transpired Jay was gay and a few years ago he exiled himself to America so as not to have to deal with breaking the news to the Mob and the endless stream of girls who were paraded before him. Navi escaped by announcing she was travelling the world and had her bags packed before having to deal with the full repercussions.

As the cab stopped outside Auntie Sheila's red front door I paid the driver and made my way nervously out. I saw

the net curtain twitch as I turned the key. Auntie Sheila
came to the door and opened it so that I almost fell in.
She looked at me coldly.

'Can't even phone me to tell me you are safe?'

'I left a message with Sasha Auntie, Ma.'

'I haven't been able to sleep, worrying if anything has
happened to you.'

This was half our problem – she wouldn't let me grow
up.

And then she hugged me. 'Why did you cut your hair?'

Auntie Sheila had brought me up from the age of five,
almost single-handedly due to the fact that my Uncle Bali
was always working. She opened this same front door all
those years ago but back then she had long, thick black
hair, large brown eyes, and appeared as a waif-like figure
that the wind could effortlessly blow over. As the years
elapsed, Auntie Sheila's figure expanded, her stomach
growing into a full moon, anchoring her and her person-
ality firmly to the ground.

When I first saw her I was taken aback as she resembled my real mother. It was like the promise of a gift being
snatched away as almost instantly I knew it couldn't possibly be her. It was in that moment that I felt the loss of my
mother, the loss of my home and all that was familiar to
me, and I comprehended somewhere that I was never going
back. I cried and I cried and I didn't stop. She tried to
console me but I didn't understand a word she was saying,

and although I could understand her gestures I chose not to acknowledge them.

Sheila came from a comfortable background and had had a convent education. She was deprived of the remainder of her scholastic years when she was presented to Dr Bali who was ten years her senior. She married him. Duty had arranged it.

Duty, she thought, was far more important than choice. Duty took someone close to a perceived happiness, and choice led to a happiness that she believed never really existed. Duty duly took care of her and brought her to England to be a doctor's wife. The couple were awaiting news on an impending birth but it never arrived. They waited and waited until fate took pity on them and brought me to their doorstep.

'The garden always has ways of producing red berries in wintertime,' she said.

Somewhere, perhaps, she was somewhat disappointed when she conceived me. The expectation, the hope, the waiting that grew in her womb was larger than herself. It was certainly larger than the five-year-old that came to her crying.

Instantly, I took a dislike to her because she was the one who provoked all those feelings of sadness in me and who took me away from my home. So at night I imagined her with her long hair like a witch and wished she would fly away on her broomstick and let me go back to my life. If

I couldn't have my grandmother then I didn't want her to look after me. Moreover, I missed my coffees in the morning. Auntie Sheila couldn't do it right – she couldn't do anything right.

My grandmother milked Ashothi the cow. The milk still warm, she would boil it, whipping in clouds to make an Indian-style cappuccino which she poured into a little steel cup so it would retain its heat, and then she would put lots of sugar in it and sprinkle crushed cinnamon over the top and present it to me.

My grandmother parcelled me up and sent me off with the same preparation she gave the coffee – in a little white outfit with a big red bow and with 'love' written all across it. Unbeknownst to me, she was sending me away, to a better fate.

I think it was a Friday because the dried-up vegetable man who sold us tomatoes and brinjals was also there. He carried them on a woven basket balanced steadily on a damp cloth on his head. The water that emanated from the cloth disguised itself as beads of sweat which he would mop up with his loin cloth.

Maybe the vegetable man knew where I was going. He wore a different, pitiful look in his eyes, not the one that said that he had not sold enough vegetables and that his wife would give him grief. I waved goodbye to them thinking that I was going on an outing to the big city to see the trains, to smell the smoke and to eat peanuts in a paper cone with this new man who I was told was my long-lost uncle. This new uncle filled the inside of the car with balloons, which had been twisted into animal shapes.

The engine roared from the big black car I sat in, emitting diesel fumes. It scared the chickens so that they screeched loudly and ran away. I laughed. Then my grandmother, who stood behind the gate, watching, removed her shawl and ran towards the car. She put the shawl through the open window, kissed my forehead, whispered some words to me and turned away. I wanted her to look back and take one of the balloon animals I held out for her, but she didn't.

I placed her shawl on my lap, thinking it meant that I would be back later that evening, and that she had told me to breathe and listen to what my heart was saying to me because the journey would take all day — and so if I got lonely, I could talk to my heart as she had shown me. I didn't return that evening, or the next. I never saw my grandmother again.

My grandfather, who has attached himself as an afterthought to the end of the feelings associated with my grandmother, was much, much bigger than this. The shape of his stomach was like my Auntie Sheila's only larger and firmer. I used to jump up and down on it as if it were my own bouncy castle and he used to bellow with delight. At least, I think it was delight. Looking back, though, it could have been excruciating agony – I really don't know.

Sometimes I hid underneath his big white loongi which was like a wigwam – the top of which he belted up tightly with a huge leather belt. My grandfather's legs were like the central pole that held the whole construction up and as the wigwam moved I would move with it. My grandmother would get very annoyed if she saw my little feet beneath his loongi and would shout at me to get out of there. It was the only time she shouted at me. She would also give him a defiant stare for allowing me to do that but she never said a word to him.

He and my grandmother stopped talking shortly after he sold his wedding ring to buy a spare part for his car. He spent most of the time polishing the old car, inside and out, and riding around frightening the villagers with the sound of the horn. He also spent a lot of his time playing cards with his friends and fighting with them. The rest of his time, he spent with me.

My grandfather used to put me to sleep with stories of the polecat who came at night to take away the chickens when they were asleep. The polecat came big and strong, the size of a monster, disguised by the night so no one knew who he was. The chickens would scream for their lives to be spared and if the polecat felt generous he would let them go, and if he was mean he would walk away with a baby chick in his mouth. I don't think my grandfather knew that this terrorised me so much. I would ask for him to sit with me, holding my hand until I fell asleep.

Out of his four daughters, my mother Nirmilla had been his favourite because he said that she brought him luck. Superstition permeated his life: if he were going somewhere in the morning and the first person he met was of an unpleasant disposition, it meant he would have an unfortunate day and he would turn right back and head for home. If the matter required some urgency and necessitated an outing, he would send my mother out and then orchestrate a meeting, pretending that he had stumbled upon her by chance. He made her do this every time, for my mother was beautiful. In his eyes, being touched by such beauty, no matter how contrived, could only bring him good luck.

I don't remember much about my mother or my father, perhaps because the little memories I have of them are so fragile. But, growing up, they have existed in my mind as the perfect parents, which my Auntie Sheila and Uncle Bali could never compete with. I do remember my mother sitting in front of a mirror and brushing out her long black hair and also that there was always music in the house and a song about a little elephant my mother sang to put me to sleep. I can also remember the day that my grandmother told me that they had gone on a very long journey and it was a journey that very special people made, and though I couldn't see them, they could see me.

At this point, my grandfather pulled out a doll he had bought for me and said he had named her Nirmilla after my mother. He bit his lip as he handed her to me; it began to bleed. Looking back, he took my mother's death really badly; and he concealed this very well. But inside his heart ticked faster and faster and nobody really knew its pain until, a few weeks after her departure, it exploded.

And as for the doll, I think I left it behind on the plane when my Uncle Bali had to carry me off kicking and screaming.

The ultimate sacrifice, the act of truly loving, is not just a physical letting go but one which encompasses all senses. It was only on that mountain-top I understood this. For a long time I resented my grandmother for letting me go. Thinking it was because she did not love me; that all those I had loved seemed to go. I imagined them all continuing their lives without me. Holding on begrudgingly to a life that could have been was a way of avoiding what really was, and, of course, a way of conserving the fairy tale that never really existed.

Still, I held on to my grandmother's shawl as I slept. Scrunching it into a ball, I slept on it, breathing her. Infused with her memory, I would be put to sleep inhaling dreams of us wading through the cow dung, laughing and milking the cows, chasing after the chickens, splashing in the muddy

54

paddy fields, grinding rice at the mill and returning home to the warm scent of incense sticks that filled our house.

One day I could not find my shawl. I looked around, searching frantically, desperately. Auntie Sheila had put it through the washing machine.

In those first years I gave my Auntie Sheila hell. My obstinate silences piercing various parts of her body, causing wounds which would only be assuaged by her invisible night tears. Some were the size of bullet holes, and no doubt the conviction with which she bore me gushed forth, provoking endless doubts as the nights passed.

At first, I'm sure it must have been duty on her part that kept her going, because I was truly unlovable. I tested her to the limit to see if she would leave me too, but then, gradually, love unmasked itself in countless ways: the way she called my name; the way she tried to learn Malayalam so she could communicate with me; the nights she would hold me tight when I cried; the day she walked up the stairs smiling and I burst into tears at seeing all the long black hair gone, a new afro haircut proudly in its place. With her long black furry coat she looked like a missing member of the Supremes.

Specifically, the day I knew I grew to love this woman who became my mother was when I was playing in the playground. I saw this figure watching me and I knew it was her. I ran over to her and she put her fingers through the fence and touched me. 'Just wanted to know that you were okay, Molu.'

The bell rang just then and I returned to my classroom. 'Was that your mum?' my friends asked.

'Yes,' I replied, and inside I was overwhelmed with pride. She was my mother and she was beautiful and kind.

This pride, however, deflated as adolescence set in. Deflate is really not the word, as I stabbed it and left it in a corner somewhere. Nobody ever explained to me that there was no point in trying to make sense of the senseless. We all could have saved ourselves a lot of pain. She wanted me to go in one direction, I wanted to go in another, and in defiant acts of rebellion, whenever she shouted at me, I said some awful things and would remind her that she was not my real mother. It was inexcusable, but deep down I still feared her leaving me too, so I did it to test her further. When we had got past that period and she still stayed with me, I thought I owed her everything and then became the person she wanted me to be.

That particular period of adolescence was characterised by Auntie Sheila's new afro hairdo. It had liberated her in the sense that she not only participated in activities with her friends, but she led them, immersing them in the countless battles to be waged. Naturally, there was dissension, but she held her troops together. She was destined to be leader of an army or a country, but fate had for some reason changed its mind, or maybe she had decided otherwise.

Our relationship – after we had salvaged ourselves from the murky waters to which we plummeted – could be characterised by alternating fear and disappointment, chasing each other like cat and mouse, though nobody really knew who the cat was and who the mouse was. Just like nobody knew who was disappointing whom, though it felt like me most of the time. I would try to please Auntie Sheila as much as I could and then I would drop a huge bombshell to undo it all.

Thinking about it now, maybe it was always this way. Like the time she sent me to classical Indian singing lessons and asked me to sing a classical love song in front of all her friends. She sat proudly; they all waited with their legs crossed underneath their saris, ready to provide the percussion with the beat of their right hands. The harmonium played 'Sa', which is middle C. I took a deep breath and began, 'Do you really want to hurt me? Do you really want to make me cry?' To which they could not keep the beat. She swiftly got up and took me home.

One of the many other big disappointments was just a week ago when I broke off my engagement to Mr Perfect, Avinash Kavan. Auntie Sheila was so devastated; she was stunned into absolute silence. She was probably irate too, wondering how I could have done something like that to her, embarrassing her in front of all her friends, after all the planning, the preparation. And here I was again, standing in her tight embrace, ready to detonate another one of her dreams.

I only consented to marrying Avinash Kavan because I was on the rebound. Uncle Bali had found him for me after I shocked everyone by saying I wanted to go the arranged route. It had only been a matter of weeks since I had broken up with Mark Dian and I couldn't handle the sense of rejection.

Mark Dian walked into my life on a rainy day outside Baker Street tube station. Bustling my way calmly through the rush hour, I almost had a fight with the lady giving out leaflets. Every morning she would push them into the commuters' hands but always dismissed mine. That morning I went up to her and grabbed one of her many leaflets that she desperately thrust onto others and that she clearly guarded from me. The lady gave me a stern look as I pulled one out of her hand.

I took the leaflet to one side and read it. Big, bold letters asking for men to try out the new barbers on Tottenham Court Road. Mark was behind me and had witnessed the whole leaflet procedure. Amused by the situation, he walked up to me. 'Good barbers, should try it out. It comes highly recommended,' he said, patting his bald head. It was a young bald head – he couldn't have been more than thirty.

Ordinarily, I would have dismissed this comment with an aversion to talking to strange men coming out from tube stations, but he was incredibly charismatic and he made me laugh on a rainy day, so I found myself engrossed in conversation.

Mark asked me on a date that same morning and told me to just call into work saying I was sick. Impressed by his audacity, this is exactly what I did. Being with him was spontaneous and exciting; he made me feel carefree and opened me up to a world of possibilities.

The relationship was filled with drama and tension because he was never predictable and I never knew what he would do next, and perhaps this is what I liked about him the most. It was made all the more intense as I knew that Auntie Sheila would never accept him.

Despite the fact that he always said he loved me, after almost a year of seeing him I summoned up the courage to tell him that I loved him and began seriously thinking about breaking the news to Auntie Sheila. A week after that he said he was going to Australia for six months. He didn't ask me to go with him. I was absolutely crushed; I thought I really loved him but perhaps it was everything that I couldn't be that made me love him more. He gave me a sense that there was much more out there, a sense of escapism from the mundane routine I had created.

Auntie Sheila was right: security and stability was everything in a relationship, love came later. I needed a secure type of love – a love with all the guarantees – so that is why I asked my Uncle Bali to find me someone.

Before getting to 'the one', Uncle Bali 'introduced' me to lots of different people. But as soon as I saw Avinash Kavan I just knew it was him. The frustrations of my entire life were placed in the sturdy hands of this man, and naively I thought that he was the perfect answer to all my problems. Within the space of being presented to him I had already married him, bought a house, and was picking out the names of our children.

'Pleased to meet you,' he said confidently as he stretched out his hand and placed mine into it.

'Yes,' I replied. Meaning that yes, I did, and all that was required was the confetti and we would be pronounced man and wife.

'He's a lawyer you know, top law firm,' insisted Uncle Bali. The way he said 'lawyer' was etched on my mind, and then he repeated it and repeated it again as if he had sat with Mr Kavan through all those years of studying, paid for him, and was trying to get his money's worth.

My Auntie Sheila and the rest of the Mob were delighted when I began seeing Mr Kavan and then elated when we formalised the situation. A whole military operation was put into place as plans were made. Amongst all the emotion, Auntie Sheila's pride shone like a beacon, radiating from her smile as she opened and closed her mouth.

Avinash and I were happy. I knew exactly where I stood

with him for he was reliable and predictable and everyone loved him.

Three months before the wedding, whilst out on my lunch break, I saw Avinash coming out of an Italian restaurant, his arms around a curly brunette. Then he kissed her, or suctioned her, for that was what his kisses were like – Hoover suctions that left me void of sentiment. He put his fingers through her curls, pressed her hand and then walked off, looking back at her several times. He never touched my hair like that or pressed my hand.

I could have excused such an incident, having talked myself into 'being in love', and just thinking of my Auntie Sheila brandishing 'duty, duty and duty', but it was the way he put his fingers through her hair that made me realise I would never be enough.

It was then I realised that trying to escape from all that I feared was pointless. It was time to grow up and take responsibility – hence the retreat into bed to think about things.

'Let me take a good look at you,' Auntie Sheila said after she released me from her clasp.

'Ma, it's only been nine days.'

'Yar, but anything could have happened. You read about all these things in the newspapers. Thank you Jesus.'

She very rarely used Jesus's name. Despite the fact that

she was a Catholic she had sort of converted to Hinduism since marrying my Uncle Bali. Jesus's name, therefore, was only brought out in desperate situations.

She then made the sign of the cross. It was only then, when her index finger pointed up to her forehead, that I noticed that her third eye was naked and realised that it was the fourteenth day of the month when all the secret rituals were practised.

The third eye is strategically placed in the centre of the forehead. A veritable power-point. The Mob concealed their power-points with a circular red sticky dot or a multi-coloured one, depending on their outfits. The secret of the eye was diligently kept until Auntie Sasha let it slip.

Auntie Sasha let many things slip. The secret of the third eye escaped many years ago in the supermarket, when Mrs Walters, one of our neighbours, asked, 'Why do yous wear 'em dots?'

Touched by such an eloquently spoken sentence, Auntie Sasha felt compelled to give her an explanation.

The dot, it appeared, housed and protected the third eye. This eye saw things that the other two missed. Mrs Walters, unimpressed by such a statement, which she had or had not listened to, walked off in search of her fish-fingers. The remaining paragraph rested uncomfortably upon Auntie Sasha's tongue and eagerly waited to make an exit. My eyebrows facilitated the process by making a request for Auntie Sasha to continue.

The third eye also recharged the mind. 'Recharging' was a ritual frequently practised together by the Mob. It meant removing their stickies and chanting for several hours behind a closed door around a candle. The candle had to be placed so it was directly in line with the third eye and, slowly, they would be hypnotised by its glowing flame. The Mob would close their eyes and the third eye would take over. The eye transported them to a place where the mind rested.

Auntie Sasha said she told her mind's eye to always imagine she was the sun. Round like a lemon cheesecake, radiant, happy and vibrant. She indulged further by informing me that Auntie Sheila saw herself as a young girl running carefree on a beach in Goa. Goa was where she was from.

'That's when she was her happiest,' Auntie Sasha informed me.

In exchange for such valuable information I was about to volunteer and exchange some gossip that I was sure she was not party to. Reflecting on the repercussions of what I was about to say, I swallowed this news as it was about to exit the tip of my tongue. I did not want to add this into the equation of an already fraught love-hate relationship.

So that particular morning, after Auntie Sheila had checked me over, I broke the news to her in a manner I knew she would comprehend.

'An actress?'

Images of a stunned fairy and a flasher were no doubt going through Auntie Sheila's mind. Then the disco beat and that dance.

'But Molu, it's all very well to dream, but dreaming is dreaming, it is not reality. If you bring your dreams into reality what do you have left? Nothing. Nowhere to escape. That is painful.'

How could I tell her that I had surmounted the barriers of fear and pain? Yes, I had fears, but they dissipated the moment I said I believed. And when I believed, I saw. I had seen the African dancer. I had already obscured the boundaries between the practical and illogical.

'Ma, I know somewhere within you will understand. Remember the time you were the happiest? Running along a beach in Goa?'

She looked at me with disbelief.

'No, Molu, you're wrong. I was happiest when Bali brought you to me and I held you in my arms for the first time.'

I wanted to cry. She had never told me this, and just to check if what she was telling me was true I double-checked that it wasn't the day she married my Uncle Bali.

She shook her head.

Auntie Sheila was Uncle Bali's second wife. I read this in a letter my Uncle Bali kept in his office. I came across it accidentally when I went to look up the word 'thrombosis' in one of his medical dictionaries. There I found it, lodged between 'thrombosis' and 'thymus'.

Thrombosis: formation of a clot of blood in a blood vessel or organ of the body.
Thymus: a gland near the base of the neck.

Uncle Bali had lost his first wife in childbirth and then the child decided to leave with her. I'm not sure if she died of a clot somewhere in her body, or perhaps even in the base of the neck. But I read the letter from a man called Raj, asking if he had finally managed to find happiness again with Sheila.

Inside this envelope was also a letter from Uncle Bali to his dead wife. It asked her to forgive him for taking her away from her family and not looking after her, and for marrying again. It ended by telling her that she would always be in his heart.

Maybe this 'other' was a person that my Auntie Sheila could not even begin to compete with. Perhaps Uncle Bali idolised her as I did my own parents, and when things got too tough he retreated into this world of perfection.

I never told Auntie Sheila about this letter, despite the fact that maybe if everything was out in the open they could talk about it, perhaps even shout down the house. But I didn't say anything because, selfishly, I always feared she might leave us, and then I wouldn't know what to do.

I'm not too sure how long after this he married my Auntie Sheila, or whether in those first years they were happy together, and why they were unable to have children. What I do know is that his sense of solitude and the lack of communication made Auntie Sheila's stomach rile, producing scathing words that she emitted from her mouth like a dragon. There was resentment at the fact that responsibility rested alone, sitting firmly on her shoulders. Or perhaps it all went much deeper than that.

Their relationship was a minefield of unexpressed emotion, a place where both feared treading. Perhaps she could not give him the love of his first wife, and the child he so wanted, and he could not share his solitude for fear of loving and losing again. Instead, they confined themselves to throwing silent grenades at each other, causing minor explosions, safely bound in the knowledge that there would be no major casualties, for they were kept together by duty. Auntie Sheila was ruled by her head, not her heart, despite the fact she had a good one.

I anticipated her disapproval and then the stern look of disappointment. I was ready to handle it. We made our way into the sitting room where all the other aunties were sitting in a circle.

'Molu is going to be an actress,' Auntie Sheila announced, to the amazement of all who were present in the room. Open jaws fell to the ground with loud gasps. It was the most opportune moment to leave: whilst the double chins were still attached to the floor, nobody could really say anything.

Auntie Sheila would no doubt have to step down as leader. An important code of conduct had been violated. The obligatory mantle of hope and expectation passed down from parent to offspring was torn to shreds in one sentence. Such a precedent created a vacuum of uncertainty, which could not be permitted. They would probably desert her, or worse, turn on her.

'Go, go do it,' she said looking at me.

Outside, winter had fallen like a heavy stone, sending ripples so that even the warmest parts were chilled. The trees felt cold in their nakedness, bearing their branches like rheumatic bones. They were waiting patiently to feel the snow upon them, to feel it melt into them and give them strength to prepare for their load. They no longer shielded the row of terraced houses and their occupants. Each house was exposed as its own political unit, each trying to conserve the peace-keeping by dictatorship, one-party rule, or whatever other methods prevailed. And even then, nobody really knew what was going on inside. Decorated with lights and masked by the festivities of the season, everyone appeared happy.

When all the excuses that have barricaded fear finally tumble down, there is nothing more to do but go forward and go do whatever you have to do, and be whoever you have to be.

SHEILA

I always thought that a problem has the grandeur of importance that you give it. This theory of mine, like so many others, was blown into a thousand pieces when they said that I could no longer have children. In fact, everything that I believed in up until that time made no sense to me. It was the day I saw my son, so little and so tiny, stillborn.

Wrapped in a soft, blue blanket, he was handed to me. My baby was lifeless but he didn't feel limp and floppy. At least, I refused to believe he did. Hoping and praying that he would awake from his deep sleep, I laid my son against my chest and began rocking him, rocking him back to life. But to no avail. When the nurse came for him I fought back the tears, kissed his forehead and told him that I was really sorry for failing him, for failing to protect and bring him safely into the world. I put up no resistance as she took my baby – I didn't deserve him.

As the doors swung back behind her, my hopes and my dreams flew away with my son and a feeling of utter despair and desolation seized me; and then it was left to putrefy inside of me as they stitched me up. My husband Bali watched. He said nothing. He did nothing and he did not cry.

He left me there and went home and cleared the house, removing every single trace that our baby had ever existed; putting all his clothes in black bin-liners, dismantling the cot and dresser. He packed the baby's things and took them to the charity shop. And then he painted a clinical white over the sunny yellow walls and closed the door behind him.

We never talk about that day; we don't even refer to it. He doesn't even know that I named our son Daniel. It wasn't a Hindu name.

They send me home as the scars are healing well, but there is pain inside of me, pain that has no physical wound, and it is compounded by a sense of solitude. I want to scream and scream and not stop; I want someone to tell me why, to understand, to tell me that it was not my fault. I oscillate between this and obsession.

The days are crammed with endless obsessing of what I know I cannot have, of what I cannot touch. The senses seem to cruelly conspire to remind me of the bittersweet smell of sickness and talcum powder: suddenly, the eyes see infants everywhere and butterflies flying around, tentatively touching the skin like the fingertips of a child. And then I think of him again and again, and have pieced together a life for him with fragments of memories that are not real.

I go into his room and can see yellow walls beneath the white paint; I can see him sleeping peacefully despite the fact that there is no cot. On good days I make sense of the senseless by telling myself that it was meant to be this way; that life goes on. Life continues, a void that I try not to fall into, sitting very much alone in the company of my husband.

A little over two years after I left the hospital, my daughter came to me. It was a cold, windy day and I was ironing upstairs, hoping to disentangle my nerves by flattening the creases in Bali's shirt. Then I heard the key in the door and Bali shouted that they had arrived. I left the iron, ran downstairs, pushing away the tears from my eyes so that our little girl would not be afraid. She stood there, motionless; her large brown eyes, almost glacial, vacantly staring back at me. I hugged her tightly and kissed her, but she did not hug or kiss me back.

Molu, 'our daughter', wore a crumpled white dress with a big red bow. She was thin, so fragile and delicate, but she had already come to us snapped in many places. She was Bali's niece. Bali had had no contact with his family until the postman brought news of his brother's and sister-in-law's deaths. The bus driver was too tired, or maybe had

had one too many toddies; maybe the bus was overcrowded, or he just could not find the brake lever in time. In any case, it killed the people standing at the front. Molu's parents were amongst them.

Molu, who followed her mother Nirmilla around, clutching the tail of her sari as if she still refused to be severed from her cord, was for some reason not on the bus that day. She did not ever find out that – to abate her guilt from being separated from her daughter – Nirmilla had bought her candies, peanuts and balloons shaped like animals. All were now lying on the roadside.

The child stayed with her grandmother. Bali received a telegram telling us this. I pleaded with him that it was a sign; that we were meant to take care of her. He said and did nothing. In desperation, I wrote to the grandmother, begging her to send us the child so that we could give her a better life. This obsession, all-consuming, resulted in insane letters sent every single day – letters which I now regret. They are added to the list of other things that I regret, but the jumbled mess of sorrys are stacked so high within me they are unable to escape.

News came again a year later. Molu's grandmother had something growing inside her and she felt it would be better if the child came to live with us, despite the fact that she had two other daughters. She felt we could give her a better start.

It was hard for all of us, very hard, so that it really is

not worth reopening old wounds. I know it was hard for Molu and so that is why, when the postman came months later with news of her grandmother's death, I did not tell her. I thought it would be easier to forget and to begin again. Naively, I thought I could begin again with a new dream.

What is a dream? Something you long for and then which comes to you in broken pieces that you spend a lifetime trying to fix? And what of the dreams you did not chase but wanted to? Do they fly away to someone else? And if everyone went chasing dreams, where would we be? What about duty? Duty that keeps us firmly grounded in reality.

And if I really open my heart, what happens to the sense of control that keeps me firmly anchored? Will I sail away? And if I do, what happens?

More pain, I suppose, and so it is that I am anchored to the present with my sense of control. It is safe and it hurts less.

I believe that this sense of control developed genetically, from my father. It is ironic how one gene suddenly decides to erupt in midlife and says, 'I am from your father; here, have me.' Then you see it developing, try not to recognise it; but the more you ignore it, the more credence you give to it. It's also strange how in life you put yourself in situations or relationships you spent a childhood trying to run away from, and despite the fact that you vow never to recreate these situations for your own children, you do so unwittingly. And so it goes on.

My parents were from the coast of middle India. Where, over generations, the strong sea breeze brought ships, sailors, pirates, missionaries, and many different cultures. When it blew British influences there, my father was truly thankful. He was a military man who worked for the British army and the only one in the town who wept when they left India. When the British came, they brought many things. Many things went missing as well, like the men conscripted from across the colonies to fight World War Two. A letter was sent from a lord as to which regiments they would be required to serve. The notice was posted on the town chapel's door and my father was amongst them.

He almost did not go as he contracted a yellow-type fever that mysteriously vanished when his colonel came to visit him. A few days later, my father polished his buttons and his boots and then left. He came back almost a year later, managing to survive World War Two despite the fact that the many he had gone with returned as half the men they were, or did not return at all.

According to my father, he had been saved by his lucky button which intercepted the bullet heading only millimetres from his heart. He would sit in the main square and dangle his lucky button for all those who had lost a loved one and craved for even the slightest information as to the last few moments of their husband, son or brother.

My grandfather, believing these stories to be true, was desperate for his daughter to marry him, and although it wasn't an arranged marriage he did everything in his power to bring them together. He was a very wealthy man and so arranged dances in the main square so that they could meet.

It wasn't that difficult for my father to fall in love with my mother, for she was beautiful and had many suitors. It was also in my father's nature to have what other people wanted. My mother must have found it more challenging as he was not the handsomest of men, but she was told he had courage and dignity and these were the things that mattered to her most.

They were married and moved into a house that my grandfather had bought for them. A solid stone white house that everyone referred to as 'The Chapel'. Just across the road in the main square stood the real chapel, painted in pale pink with two enormous palm trees standing on either side. A year later, I arrived – my father did not even feign interest when he saw me and was resentful that someone else had entered the house and diverted the unfaltering attention my mother had paid him. When my sister Sasha was born fifteen months later, he grew even more petulant. In order to keep the peace my mother became more and more submissive and turned increasingly to God, who filled the void inside her.

All the memories I have of my mother are connected to God: she seemed to spend an inordinate amount of time with Him. Admittedly, she took care of us, fed, clothed and bathed us, but she was always elsewhere. Mentioning His name whenever she could, we were never allowed to forget that God was the most important member of our family, and every Sunday we went to see Him. My mother would dress my sister and me in our best clothes and take us into the real chapel where we would pray for our souls to be cleansed and left pristine like my father's boots. She would count her rosary beads with military precision so by the time she was a third of the way around, the priest would automatically look up and begin the Lord's Prayer.

Though God had an enormous presence in our house, it was my father who ran it, and he did so in a regimented manner: at precisely six o'clock in the morning he blew his bugle to awaken us and assigned my sister and me relevant household tasks which he would subsequently inspect. There would always be some form of punishment because the tasks were never completed correctly – we were never good enough.

It was impossible to please him – I learned this when I was seven and made him some tea, taking it carefully up to him. My father took a sip, looked at me and spat it out, pouring the contents of the steel cup onto the floor. He then asked me to lick it up. Standing over me as he attempted to humiliate me, I closed my eyes and did as he said. After that I stopped trying, and sometimes I wished that a tragedy would befall him. Sensing God's disapproval I would be repentant and go to confession to purify my thoughts. My sister Sasha was different; she would do anything for his approval and she would try harder, and this endeared her to him.

My father did not work but lived off a pension provided by the army and mostly off the money my grandfather had left us. This money was squandered in the square as he played cards, or on lavish family banquets held at Christmas and Easter. It was an opportunity for him to invite his friends and relatives round and you could be certain that that lucky-button story would come out. At which point my mother would make the sign of the cross and we would have to give thanks that he had been mercifully spared.

We became party to my father's warfare skills when an intruder broke into our house in the middle of a hot summer's night. I heard someone stirring downstairs and ran to my parents to alert them. My father promptly assumed his leadership responsibility and assigned me and my mother to investigate the situation. I believe this was to give him time to put on his uniform, which would help him with a strategy requiring timed dexterity. In the meantime, my mother had hit the assailant with one of her frying pans.

When all the commotion died down and all that could

be heard was my mother's laughter, my father ran down-stairs, sat on top of the intruder's body and finished him off with a few cold, hard slaps to the face. My mother just stood and watched; her laughter dissipated as she lowered her head, stepped backwards and let him take centre stage. It was a posture she adopted throughout their married life. In this respect, there is nothing more I can really tell you about my mother except that she walked around as his shadow and that she had several conversations with God; so it was only He that really knew her.

Sasha and I went to the convent not too far from our house, which was run by Sister Eugenia. Although the convent had even more rules and regulations, I loved going there as it was a way of escaping from our father. Nearly all the girls in our town went there, but if you asked in our neighbourhood who I was, everyone knew. Notoriously known as The Sinner, I unbraided my hair and ran wild through the corridors with the nuns chasing me, praying for the salvation of my soul, which they said had already escaped. Sister Eugenia urged me to pray in her presence, and Sister Maria nodded, but when Sister Eugenia left, Sister Maria said my soul was there, shining so brightly that it was too painful for the eye to see.

The first time I was introduced to her, I was six. Sister Maria had a kind, round face and wore a wimple tightly pulled over her eyebrows. I used to wonder what she had beneath it. I imagined her bald and then I imagined her with short, untidy hair; so one day as I sat with her, I just pulled it off. She had long black hair that made her face look even more beautiful. Instead of reprimanding me, as all the others did, she simply sighed.

'Aye, aye, things are going to be difficult for you, my little one.' And with that she hugged me tightly, pouring all her warmth, compassion and belief into me.

She nurtured me – attempting to redirect all the misplaced energy by urging me to sing in the choir or act in school plays. And despite the fact that I wanted to sing out of tune or had the impulse to improvise, I never did, because when I was with her I caught a glimpse of God. Not the God that they incessantly filled my days and years with, but the timeless presence of unconditional love.

As I reached my teenage years you could be sure that if there was a fight it would be me who instigated or finished it. Amongst the cheering of all the other girls, my sister Sasha would watch quietly, innocently, and would then run home and tell my father how badly I had behaved. I understand now why she did this for she craved any kind of attention from my father, but it hurt me more than anything he ever did.

The moderate control which he exercised with his belt would leave bruises that were quickly healed by the approval of my friends. He was unable to humiliate me or break my spirit and I just showed more defiance – the wildness inside of me could not be tempered and then the next day there would be another episode, and so it would go on. This pattern changed when I was fifteen, and not because of what he did to me but because of a boy called Rodrigo Fernandez.

Rodrigo was seventeen when he and his family moved in two doors away from us. I noticed him instantly whilst he was helping his father unload their possessions. It was his smile I spotted first – very warm, tender and genuine like Sister Maria's. My sister Sasha, sensing something stirring in me, said that he had smiled at her. I appeared disinterested.

Rodrigo went to the school across from the convent and one day we bumped into each other on our way home. He knew my name as he had heard my father shouting it from beyond the walls. I wondered what else he could have heard.

Despite the fact that I liked him, I remained aloof, answering all his questions monosyllabically. When I got home I thought about him. Rodrigo said he had heard about the episodes at school and asked me why. Nobody had ever asked me why. I'd like to say it was because I was wild but perhaps it was not this. It was to show that no matter what was happening on the inside, my spirit had to show that it was strong. He made me answer the questions I did not want to ask myself and he made me face the feelings of rejection my father provoked in me.

Rodrigo chipped away, and every day at four o'clock he would wait for me outside the convent. Secretly, I was desperate for the bell to ring so I could see him and walk home with him. It wasn't just the physical attraction; he expanded my world by talking to me about all the possibilities that existed beyond our town. He made me want to study harder so I could share my ideas with him; he made me like myself. And as the months passed, despite the fact that each of us knew there was something very strong between us, we never touched each other or held hands. Perhaps we should have, because maybe we could have diffused the energy that was mounting.

My mother liked Rodrigo as his family were also devout Catholics, and she invited him home when my father wasn't there. My father had seen us walking in the town together but surprisingly hadn't said or done anything. To my absolute amazement, my father even consented when Rodrigo asked him if he could take me to the Christmas dance in the town square.

I feared loving him, I mean truly loving him, and although I was nervous and excited at the prospect of him taking my hand at the dance, it made me feel sick inside. As I put on my green chiffon dress, my sister sat on my bed watching me. I combed my hair, over and over again, and then tied it up in a bun. Rodrigo came for me at exactly the time he said he would.

But we didn't go to the dance. A bus had stopped outside the chapel; it was going to the sea, and he saw me stare at it, looked at me and we both jumped on. On that journey we did not speak to each other but understood each other perfectly.

It was evening when we arrived; the air smelled of the fish that the fishermen had hauled, the moon glistened against the waves and the sea beckoned. I leaped off the bus before it stopped properly, took my shoes off, untied my hair and ran and ran along the beach. Rodrigo ran behind me, laughing because he was unable to catch up. And then, with my best clothes on, I swam into the sea. Rodrigo called out and kept calling my name until I could not hear it.

As I swam, the energy of the waves invigorated every part of my body and I no longer felt cold inside; something was lit inside of me and made me feel completely alive. I swam back to the beach and found Rodrigo sitting there with his head in his hands and tears streaming down his face.

I touched his face; he moved my hand away and shook his head. He got up, turned around and grabbed me, promising that he would never let me out of his sight again. And then he kissed me and I allowed myself to love him.

We lit a fire on the beach and sat in each other's arms,

and for the first time I had nothing to prove to anyone because somebody else loved me, and they loved me for who I was.

It was me who insisted that he go away to university and not waste his time waiting for me. He took much persuading and would leave only after I promised to write every day, which is what I did. We had made plans, confident plans to remain together until he finished. He was studying to be an engineer and I was going to train to be a teacher and then we could get married.

I am still unsure whether this sort of love is sustainable and comes from the naivety of youth, but I kept writing and believing as he did, avidly ripping open the letters he sent, smelling the musty scent of them, detecting the traces of him and devouring every word he wrote. I was filled with the illusions that naivety brings. You think you know it all.

One day the letters suddenly stopped. I waited anxiously for the postman every day, some days I pretended that I was too sick to go to school, but there was nothing. Weeks went by; I wrote frantically. Sasha said that perhaps he had found someone else, for girls his own age would be much more appealing. Weeks later, out of total desperation, I went to see his mother and asked her if this was the case. She nodded.

My heart was telling me to go to North India and see Rodrigo. This is what I desperately wanted to do. Find him and at least ask him why. Why he had given me hope, why he had made empty promises that he could not keep. But I didn't listen to my instincts because I was too proud.

I've learned only now that pride is not a good thing – it creates self-imposed obstacles. Maybe it comes from a sense of self-importance, or perhaps the complete opposite – the realisation that you are not important at all.

I was too proud in case I heard it from Rodrigo's own mouth that he did not love me; too proud to admit how much he meant to me. And so I stayed where I was and my life shrank back to the regimented ways of the chapel and I carried on as normal; I did not allow myself to crumble or even cry. Every time I was beaten I never let it show and showed defiance instead. This time was no different. Something extinguished in me as my thoughts turned to practicalities – ways in which I could leave the town and begin again.

I have never since felt the passion or the energy that I did back then – that I could do anything, be anyone. I don't know if this is what youth brings, and then as each age mounts it erases something of this passion until finally there is nothing left.

Now, sitting here in my nice, neat, quiet sitting room with the core of who I really am and forty-seven years layered upon me, I think that this is what happens if you don't do what you truly believe in: life drains and dissipates the spirit so anything becomes acceptable. Fear sets in and you explain away things by saying that that is the way they were meant to be. Anything else seems an impossibility. Such an impossibility that the mind switches itself off, leaving you to cope with a heart that knows better, and then eventually, over time, the heart's voice gets lost somewhere in the monotony of an everyday routine.

Around about this time when Rodrigo had left, my father was heavily in debt. He had gambled most of my grandfather's money away and so people started coming to The Chapel. They first came for our 'classical English furniture'. I did not know this at the time, but in a bid to keep them at bay, my father had placed an advertisement in the paper for wealthy suitors in exchange for me – his eldest daughter.

Two weeks before my seventeenth birthday, Bali came into my life.

Nobody really knew much about Dr Bali; who he was or where he came from. The investigative stage of the whole marriage process was bypassed due to the fact that my father required money and quickly. Bali was also a doctor and this was good enough for my father. The fact that he was a Hindu no longer bothered him as money had become far more important, whereas before, he treated them, if it is possible to do so, worse than the Untouchables. No questions were asked as to why a Hindu from Kerala would want to marry a Catholic girl from Goa when he had a whole southern state to choose from.

To everyone's astonishment I agreed to see him, so in this way I was not coerced. Thinking back, though, perhaps I consented to seeing Bali to test my mother, to see if the inexcusable inertia that she was in would suddenly stir to life and protect me from all that I had wanted her to protect me from; or perhaps to show Rodrigo that he could not possibly affect me.

Bali came, knocking on the Chapel door.

The day that I first saw Bali I saw the sunburned complexion of his skin and the shiny baldness of his head; this is what struck me the most as it did not equate with such a youthful face. He was dressed in a blue suit that appeared too big for him and he must have been hot and uncomfortable wearing it. As I handed him his tea, his fingers accidentally brushed against mine. I felt nothing, just inertia, but searched instead for things that I could appreciate about him, like the way he tenderly took the cup and saucer from my hands. I wanted to see signs of kindness and so noted the intonation when he said, 'Thank you'. It seemed so sincere next to my father, who took his cup and said the same empty words. And despite the fact that my father was there and had told me quite specifically not to tell him that I wanted to be a teacher, I did. Bali acknowledged this and asked me lots of questions about my favourite subjects. He didn't have the same sparkle that Rodrigo had in his eyes, or the enthusiasm for life that had exuded from him. But that was good – such things only led to false promises. Bali was a man who knew what he wanted and Rodrigo was a boy who thought he did. Bali could provide security.

As I am writing this, I realise now that it is pointless to try and control outcomes just to escape pain or to create a feeling of security to avoid further pain, because fate always has other plans, which it unravels in due course.

My father did most of the talking, answering most of the questions directed at me. Bali and I exchanged very few words, and, based on what my father had said, we signed and sealed our fate.

I wrote to Rodrigo, telling him that I was going to get married, hoping somewhere perhaps that he would come for me. No letter came back.

It was then I threw myself fully into the prospect of being Bali's wife. I could escape my father's control, my mother's submission, and begin a new life in Southern India. They had some of the best universities there. He appeared to be a kind man and that was what was most important.

I was left alone to deal with the wedding preparations and immersed myself in this, not actually thinking about the day itself when I would become Bali's wife. My mother did not help me with anything, her conversation reduced to answering only the questions asked, and on the day of my wedding she refused to get out of bed. It was the only time my mother showed defiance in her life. She did not attend my wedding, not because she wanted me to think twice about marrying him but because she felt God would not approve. It was to be a Hindu wedding and not in the sanctity of our church with the blessing of our Lord, so she stayed at home instead with her rosary beads, consoling herself, and had another conversation with God which I was not privy to. I don't know if she asked Him if she should come for me and I don't know if He answered or what He replied. The fact is, she did not come. And nobody else came to stop the wedding.

My father stood proudly, dressed in full military attire alongside my sister Sasha, who came in her school uniform. Discreetly in the corner sat Sister Maria, but I saw her, her eyes bursting with tears. There was really none of Bali's family there, only a cousin named Raj who need not have come as he hid himself beneath a bushy beard and kept looking down at his feet.

I sat behind my make-up and the thick red veil of my sari, unaware of the full implications of what I was doing. Accompanied only by a feeling that it was too late, too late to take off the veil and run wildly through the town. And yes, if I am truthful, through my veil I caught a glimpse of the African dancer, but he was dancing in another direction and it was too late, so I did not chase him.

After the wedding we travelled down south on a road with green paddy fields on either side. The workers on both sides stopped pulling out the rice and waved at us, wishing us luck. The driver sounded his horn back at them in acknowledgement, to which they began chasing the car. Coconut trees carved out a route for us and led us to a huge blue mountain which touched the sky.

As we drove, I left The Chapel and the past behind me, believing that I could make this marriage work – we could find common ground. A lasting love probably came from friendship – and Kerala, from everything I had read, was a beautiful place to start again. More than any other state in India it allowed women access to education, and this was what I had buried myself in since Rodrigo's departure.

We stayed in a hotel in a place near Trivandrum – a stopover, I thought, before continuing further south to the village where Bali was from. We would meet his parents, enjoy the festivities of being newly married and then begin our new lives. The next day we woke up very early with the sunshine beaming down upon our faces. We got up and continued our journey. To my absolute shock, we took a plane and flew to London.

So, the love that they speak of, the passion that is the subject of so many books and films; I felt it momentarily but it didn't last and so I chose to believe that a lasting love cannot exist in this form. That is the land of fairy tales and my heart is grounded firmly in reality.

I remember going through a long tunnel at Heathrow airport. Coming out from the other end I was greeted with a big yellow sign in bold black letters – 'Welcome to London'. Bali had bought me woollen cardigans to wrap around my sari blouse. I refused to wear them and even if I had put them on it still would not have prepared me for the cold I was to encounter – it is the kind of cold that seeps into your bones and is able to dampen the spirit. The little hope that was left within me was completely blown away. As my mother had taught me – you accept your situation and get on with whatever needs to be done.

Number 74 Conrade Gardens was our home for the first two years. It was a tiny little bedsit on top of an English takeaway which we shared with some mice who occupied the property. If you sat on the sofa and went to retrieve whatever had been lost amongst the cushions you could feel the furry things squealing in the palm of your hands. At first I just wanted to scream; then I wanted to squeeze them dead in my hand.

We had to heat that place up by putting ten-pence pieces into the electric meter, and for some reason it would go cold again in the middle of the night and the dampness that surrounded us became even more acute. On the weekends I would take our clothes to the launderette and sit there for hours, watching them spin, dirty stains cleaned by a monotonous Sunday. After they were washed I would load them into two black bin-bags and then bring them home again, weighing twice their original weight. Hanging the damp clothes out wherever I could find space, still coldness – damp coldness.

The everlasting noise of loud music playing, ceaseless drumbeats that would play in my head day and night. The horrible smell of what I now know to be fish and chips, wrapped in soggy newspaper. To escape, I would walk and walk. Sandals, socks and sari on grey pavements, met with unaccustomed stares, cold and unwelcoming, occasionally interjected with a 'go back to where you came from'. But I would walk and dream that I was free, running along a beach with my hair untied – full of hope and possibility.

Every now and then, letters from home would arrive – sealed with the smell of leftover rice cakes from my mother who was still praying for me. Sasha would say that things were not the same without me, and my father would end it by scribbling his signature and spelling out his full name.

I would save from my housekeeping money and send them a postal order to show them how well I was doing and a long letter telling them how very happy I was, and then I would write a few words in Bali's hand as if he were really there with me.

Bali was busy finishing his medical training. At this stage I didn't know that he was not a doctor yet. Just another one of those things that I didn't know about him. If Bali was not at college he was in the library, and if he was not in the library he was at the hospital. I immersed myself in reading books from the library and escaping through other people's imaginary worlds but then, after I finished them, the starkness of where and who I was became even more acute. Then I took to reading facts, facts that I could not share with anyone, meaningless facts about countries I would never visit or famous people in history who were dead.

Nothing I can tell you now will capture the moment of how I felt back then. Placed in a culture that I did not understand – amidst jumpers for the teapots, electric meters, ten-pence pieces and the cold, cold wind – I felt bereft of illusion and at the total mercy of time, just willing something better, waiting for just one New Year to come and sweep me off my feet. I imagined and dreamed of this and then it finally came.

* * *

A new start finally came as we moved to a house in the suburbs. A little three-bedroom with a big garden; nice, polite neighbours with white net curtains; and news that I was pregnant. I can say that our marriage only really began when I told Bali this news. He wept with delight and held my hand saying he would do anything to look after me and the baby and that we would want for nothing. He made me feel safe.

My hopes for the future grew with this child inside me, as did the affirmation that I had not been wrong and that I had chosen correctly. It was the first time that I really began to love Bali. He made time for me and would come home earlier with flowers, and chocolates wrapped in gold foil. He made me feel wanted, telling me to rest; he would caress my feet and call me tender names. All these things filled me once again with a love that got bigger as our child grew inside of me.

I thought I got to know Bali; the Bali on the inside who was generous in spirit and who did whatever he could for others. I got to know that he didn't work every hour so he could avoid coming home to me but worked because he was passionate about his vocation and wanted to do everything he could to help his patients.

Bali and I were deciding on names for our baby. I wanted to give the baby a Hindu name and for it to grow up knowing about Hindu traditions, not with the rules and regulations I had been brought up with and fearing God was forever watching his every move. Bali was taken aback, and that is how we decided on the names Arujan for a boy and Shamilla for a girl.

I knew that we would have a boy.

I talked to this baby who had rented his space inside of me: when he kicked or when I felt his sharp elbow pound against my stomach, when he asked me to eat olives in a chilli hot sauce. We listened to music and read stories together. I told him how life would be and how we would take care of him, and sometimes we would be very angry with him as he would be with us, but we would take care of that too. For life was like that. But most of all, I vowed to do what my mother had not done: I would protect him and make sure nothing bad ever happened to him.

I wrote to my parents telling them when the baby was due – my mother sent a letter saying that God would forgive me if the child was baptised and ended by saying that she would send Sasha to help me. My father said nothing.

We prepared the room upstairs in a pale yellow with wallpapered borders with a duck print, and then we bought a wardrobe, dresser and cot to match.

Then one July day as we sat down to eat, my waters broke and I nodded to Bali. With happy, nervous anticipation we drove quickly to the hospital and I was fitted with a white gown that covered the contractions that took over my whole body. Bali paced outside for hours.

Nothing really prepares you for pain like that. Acute and relentless, spasmodic, time just to catch enough breath to push. I pushed with all the effort that has been my life. Gasping and crying for the strength of an unrhythmic breath that was short and erratic. Enveloped in delirious heat that made the labour even more unbearable, struggling as I pushed, thinking that this was beyond anything I could do. No more; I gave up.

Then, something came from deep within me; I don't know exactly from where but it was like an enormous wave that pushed and guided my baby from within me. I screamed with a sense of release.

A calm sigh of relief followed and a huge smile spread across my face as I turned to look at my baby. Silence. No cries of entering new light. I looked across. He was blue – a stillborn dream. I did not protect him, or perhaps I was not worthy of him, so he left me there, alone.

My sister Sasha had been sent by my mother to help me with the birth of my son but as soon as she arrived, she left to go in search of the greener pastures of England.

Bali went to look for her to tell her the news and bring her back to be with me. He found her somewhere on a hippy trail, finding the meaning of life in a caravan park with a man from Port Talbot. She did not manage to attend the funeral as she was too high on some substance of love. When she threw her arms around me and told me how incredibly sorry she was, all I felt was indifference.

Sasha would sit at the edge of my bed and would fill the time with endless chatter which I never listened to – not until she mentioned the name Rodrigo Fernandez. I turned my head towards her and asked if he was well. She informed me that he had got married shortly after hearing I was pregnant. I let her carry on.

He had married Frances, one of Sasha's friends. They had met last year when Rodrigo had come back. He had asked after me, and Sasha, producing one of my letters, had told him I was happily married to Bali and was living in England. It was then he had said to her how he couldn't understand why I had left him.

It didn't make sense. I was feeling too numb and dazed to ask, but Sasha continued.

After some investigating, she had found out that our father thought the only way out of his financial predicament was if he married me off, so after he had placed the advertisement he intercepted all the correspondence between Rodrigo and me. He then went to see Rodrigo's mother, saying there would be no way he would accept a union between both families and so the best thing, if I came to ask, was to say that Rodrigo was not interested any more. He wrote to Rodrigo in my hand, telling him I had fallen in love with someone else.

A lump formed in my throat and tears rolled down my face. He had loved me and I hadn't had the courage to follow my heart and go and see him for fear of his rejection. And now this rejection had followed me to a suburb in London and crawled inside of me and sat in the place where my son was – a big black hole that nobody could fill – not even my husband, who had no words for me.

I began to scream and scream and I could not stop. I wanted to be wherever my son was. The doctor came to sedate me and prescribed sleeping pills and antidepressants to take the pain away.

That year passed me by.

Molu came and occupied that void and made me feel again. She came and took that empty white space upstairs, filling it with her laughter, her moods, her temper and her spirit.

I know now the easiest thing to be in the world is a bad mother. Just because you are a mother, you don't know it all. To be a good mother is the hardest thing of all. A world full of paradoxes. You want to give your children the wings to fly away but you also want to clip them so you can keep them safely at home. You want them to love you unconditionally but you know that there are always things that they will blame you for. You want to give them everything but you can't, because you know that isn't the way the world works.

A Sindy doll, a strange-looking thing with no weight or hips, is what Molu kept asking me for. She was blonde with very long legs. I didn't want to buy it. To explain to a child why you don't want to buy it is difficult. What do you say – a self-image like that is detrimental to the psyche? Maybe I should have bought it but I went to the market and bought her a nice plump doll with ginger curls whom I called Sindy.

To see the disappointment made my stomach churn, but you know I had to be firm; you can't always give in, even if you want to, even if it hurts. This is how it always felt in the early years – that she was so very disappointed in me. This is how it has always felt – until now. The disappointment was combated on my part with the stance of ever-increasing firmness. Sometimes, when you don't know how to handle a situation, you do the exact opposite of what you intended to do; and you put so much energy into trying to control it that it takes on a life of its own and goes the other way.

I was always so very proud of her. The spirit she had was the embryo of the once-upon-a-child that was me. I watched her play the Virgin Mary who then hit the innocent Joseph as she looked at a plastic, bald-headed doll that she knew could not belong to either of them and then threw it out of the crib. The other parents gasped in horror at the unruly child. But inside, my laugh was so uproarious that it looked as if I was going to be sick.

I had to reprimand her though. To let the spirit grow uncontrollably is to send it to a difficult place where the unexpected boundaries of reality are too painful. I thought it would be best to set her in the discipline and sanctity of a culture that would keep her safe. It is the common ground of conformity and security – what has always been.

A child needs discipline and roots, otherwise it goes searching for a sense of self, something elusive, something that is not there. Even if they rebel against the stability that you have endeavoured to give them, this is good – for you can only rebel if you know who you are and where you came from – but to rebel against nothing, to wander aimlessly feeling that there is something missing, is hard.

This is why I brought her up in the sanctuary of the Hindu culture, despite the fact that I had been brought up a Catholic and did not speak her language. When she first came I sought out Malayalam classes where I could learn and asked Bali to speak to me in Malayalam when the two of us were alone together. This is how I first got Molu to smile at me as I pointed to things and mispronounced them. She would teach me; I wanted to learn from her.

I never knew if she would love me back but this wasn't the most important thing to me when she first came. It was the feeling of being able to do something that could make a difference and the feeling of being needed; life seemed to make sense. Things changed when she began loving me. She had been with us for four months before she put her arms around me and kissed me. We had spent the day making puppets out of socks and buttons and then we put on a puppet show for when Bali came home. When it was time for her to go to bed, I kissed her on the fore-head and she grabbed my neck and kissed me back. I wanted to cry and I suppose that is when fear set in. Love had entered into the equation, and with love there is always much at stake.

When I felt she was comfortable with Bali and me, we decided to send Molu to school. The first day I took her I hid behind a tree and watched her play by herself. She wasn't a shy child, she was just cautious having been through much upheaval. In spite of the fact that I knew she would eventually make friends, I willed for someone to go and talk to her, and when after three days she was still sitting on her own I took matters into my own hands. Despite the fact that it wasn't her real birthday, I organised a party and began talking to some of the mothers so that they would bring their children.

It's sometimes hard to know when to take control and when to let go and let things take care of themselves. The children loved the clown, and the day after when I went to school and watched from behind the tree, Molu was play-ing with a little girl. But it wasn't a girl who had come to the party.

Bali laughed when I told him this and said that in this respect she was just like Kurmilla, her aunt. Caught unaware, he smiled, reminiscing in a way that I had never seen him do before. His face completely softened and relaxed; it was like a window that had been previously shut had opened, and it was only he who was party to what lay behind it. He never talked about his past. Before meeting me, he said he hadn't had much of a childhood and was sent away to work and then did everything to make sure he had a better life. I wanted to know more about this aunt, more about what had happened to her. As I probed further I remember feeling distinctly uncomfortable because of the way Bali was acting. He abruptly ended the conversation by telling me that she was dead. Maybe I should have asked him if there was something he wanted to tell me, but I didn't, perhaps fearing it was something that I didn't want to hear.

Our relationship improved greatly when Molu came into our lives because we no longer had to focus on each other – what he did or did not say to me did not seem to matter as it was about someone else now. Bali spent most of the week at the hospital, working so that he could provide for everything she could possibly want, and the weekends the three of us would spend as a family, either going on outings or meeting with other friends who had children. Perhaps for our own selfish reasons, all our energy was invested into this child, our unfulfilled hopes and aspirations placed upon her. Did we spoil her? We probably did. Trying to overcompensate and give her the things we never had. Even then, we got it wrong.

After school I'd take her to dance classes and classical Indian music classes which she appeared to love. However, in a recital that had been organised so I could show off her talents, she looked me straight in the eye and sang some words asking if I really wanted to hurt her. My friends looked at me, astounded. Instead of telling her then that all I had ever wanted to do was to protect her, I marched her off home, too proud to tell her anything because she had made me feel inadequate. Nothing I did could ever be good enough – it was a pattern that was to follow me throughout my life, from my father, from my mother, my husband and my daughter. I know now that what you fear becomes you; you make the very circumstances you try to avoid happening.

Bali took charge in these situations – the only time he ever did – and would try to explain to Molu why I did the things I did, but he didn't even know so he never made a good job of it.

He was a good father to her in the sense of what a good father means to our generation. This was to protect and provide and to do his duty. Nowadays, to be a good father you have to be their friend. You have to buy their awful music and pretend to enjoy it with them.

What is that funky music of youth trying to express? An energetic rhythmic beat, trying to provoke all those dormant thoughts. How bizarre life is, that now all this music, bindis, saris, chicken tikkas and thablas are 'in'.

Twenty years ago 'Asian underground' was when we were scared of going out, and stayed in with the fear of finding a petrol bomb with our morning post.

Only the most adventurous would have Tupperware parties, and the most defiant would have an Avon lady come around and display her goods. In the beginning, I never held such events, never even went to them as I didn't know where to go and had nobody to go with.

My busy days were filled with cleaning the house, shopping, making Bali's dinners and then picking Molu up from school. One day when we got home I noticed that Molu wasn't wearing the right coat. It had the name Navi sewn onto the label. Navi was the girl who had begun playing with Molu at school. There was a telephone number stitched meticulously beneath her name. I dialled the number and the lady who answered the phone was to become my very good friend – Asha.

She invited me to her home. The moment she opened the door there was an instant recognition; she had a round face like Sister Maria's, which was lit by a kind smile. I knew that it would be a friendship that would endure. They are very rare, these orchestrated moments when you meet someone for the first time and feel you have spent a lifetime with them. In the space of a few hours, as our children played together upstairs, we were able to share secrets of a past and hopes and fears of a future.

I told her about my first love, how I had met Bali, the loss of my son and how Molu had come into our lives. Asha told me about having to get married and coming to England with two small children, Jay and Navi, and the loveless marriage she was in. We understood each other's disappointments and tried to find meaning in them. It was a relief for me to talk to someone, someone who could understand.

Maybe it is just an overwhelming solitude that does this. The soul magnetically radiates to another of its kind, then unburdens itself and seals its secrets in the boundaries of a friendship. These boundaries are pulled in so many directions and tested over time.

Every day, after school, Asha and her children would either come to my house or we would go to hers. As our children played we would cook together and talk. Sometimes we listened to Indian music, dancing around the kitchen and laughing at our own insanity. In more serious moments, Asha taught me how to sit calmly, candle-gaze and meditate. It was unnerving at first as my mind had problems focussing, flitting between one thing and another, but she held my hand and talked me through it, asking me to remember one of the happiest times in my life when I felt completely free. Often the images would be of a young girl in a green chiffon dress running along the beach. I wanted to reach that girl and tell her things but she would run away. It would often end with me in tears but Asha would squeeze my hand – there was someone else in my life now, helping me fight. Something I hadn't felt in a very long time.

I wish, though, that someone had told me that surrendering was equally if not more important than fighting.

Asha wanted to introduce me to her circle of friends and invited me to her friend Meena's Tupperware party. Meena lived a few streets away in a large house. She was dressed in an elegant sari and eyed me suspiciously as she opened the door. It was the kind of suspicion that wanted to know what was so special that made her friend talk about me so much.

It transpired that Meena had not lived too far from the town I had in Goa, and her husband was also a doctor. It was a strange coincidence, as he knew Bali well, but it wasn't one of those coincidences that made me warm towards her. Quite the opposite – she asked lots of questions and acted as if she knew something I didn't. As the evening progressed, out of politeness, I made an effort with her.

The party began with women passing the containers around, inspecting them and then making amusing comments about their shapes. It wasn't about containers but about a group of women who congregated together under a pretext and who found common bonds. They sat eating, talking, drinking orange juice, laughing at the shapes of the containers in such an uncontrollable manner that you could not help but be affected.

As we made our way out, Meena said it was a pleasure meeting me and hoped that all of us could get together with our husbands soon. Perhaps I had judged her too hastily, it was just her manner to present a cold exterior – and in this respect, she reminded me a little of myself.

When I arrived back home I asked Bali how he knew Meena and her husband Govinder, and attempting to brush over the topic he said that he had met Govinder whilst he was doing his training. He reluctantly agreed to the invitation to have dinner with them and Asha and her husband Amit.

It was only that second time I met her that I actually warmed to Meena. She seemed less wary of me and much more accepting. She talked about Goa and we laughed at the same idiosyncrasies that we had brought from there, such as walking with an umbrella through London when it was hot to protect us from the sun. When her defences were down she was a warm person.

From that day, Asha, Meena and I did everything together, and on the weekends we would organise outings for the children and our husbands would join us. In those earlier days we watched our children play and fight each other, we exchanged clothes and recipes and problems. There was, inevitably, the strange dynamic that comes with being part of three – but we managed, laughing, crying or fighting our way through.

The core of our friendship, the complicity of sharing exactly the same experience at exactly the same time, wrapped with compassion and love, is now buried under twenty layers of changing circumstances and reactions to those circumstances. We were unable to sustain communication in many of those moments, so we just pretended that things were as they always were, if not better.

If I am honest, I felt betrayed by both of them. There were things I told Asha that she shared with Meena and things that Meena would use against me. She would analyse the imperfections of my relationship with Bali because her relationship with her husband was floundering; she would make insinuations which at the time made no sense to me. She made comparisons between her children and my own child, and instead of asking her what was wrong and finding the source of her insecurity, I made her feel as inadequate as she was making me feel.

Being amongst each other did not feel right; nothing felt right and things that we had said for years, or mannerisms we had always had, were cause for irritation on all sides. So we said nothing, leaving those unsaid words somewhere inside, left alone to play with our assumptions. And when our children were grown, we had lost the glue that had held us together.

Now, I do not understand why we would intentionally want to inflict pain on each other, but this is what we did. Consequently it has made us drift further apart, with each of us desperately clutching at a raft of friendship that has degenerated considerably.

When you see you are losing something else that is so important to you, you lose the sobriety of a contented heart. So instead of letting go, trusting in love, I took control, providing security and leadership, waging them in the countless battles I did not really believe in, internal dissension masked by attacking and gossiping about others. It was the best way of concealing an ever-increasing insecurity. If I am now to take responsibility for what I did, I would say that I polluted it with a bitterness I was unable to communicate. Meena and Asha had known things about Bali that they could have told me about, at least prepared me for. For their part, they allowed our friendship to be contaminated with their silence.

What has happened to these friendships now is that there is a hollow shell and nothing left. The sad thing is, I think that every one of us knows this. So we engage in our superficial conversations and parade around as if we are better and happier, because we know that if we really look beyond this, we will find that there is nothing left.

Even with my sister Sasha, if you look beyond the sibling tie, there is nothing there. I love her because of duty and obligation but fail to see the amusing side of her that makes other people laugh. My sister came in and out of my life, taking with her the best of things and walking away when things got hard. She had come to help me with the birth of my son and ended up staying.

Sasha decided she wanted to train to be a nurse. Bali helped her, even finding her nursing quarters. She would come and visit us when she needed to, using our home as a base as she jumped from relationship to relationship. The only reason I allowed her to stay was because Molu loved her so much, but after months of being there she would grate on me. When she wanted to buy a flat of her own, Bali helped her with a deposit and she found somewhere not too far away from us.

My mother had died around the time Molu first came to us so I could not go and attend her funeral. All the emotions that came to me in the aftermath were suppressed as I tended to my own daughter. My father joined her seven years ago, but for me he died a long time before that so I was unaffected by the news and just noted the irony that he had had a long and protracted life and died peacefully in his sleep. Whilst he was alive, I sent him a postal order every month which he never acknowledged. He would write to Sasha instead, giving news of his various ailments and how close to death he was. Sasha went to India to visit him a few times.

There would be so many things that I would be bursting to ask her – like if he had asked after me, if the real chapel was still painted pink, if she had bumped into Sister

Maria or seen Rodrigo – did he have children? But I didn't ask her anything and, unusually, she did not volunteer this information. After my father died, he left her The Chapel, which she subsequently sold.

Sasha did not marry, nor have children, and she embarrassed me when she bounced into the room where we sat in the company of friends. She was loud and her laughter irritated me. You may think that I resented her for doing all the things I was unable to do, for being the daughter that my father loved, but you would be wrong. It wasn't this.

It's about seeing it through together when things are hard and about loyalty and commitment. I don't mean a physical presence, but knowing at the end of the day that you are there for each other. I never felt this from her. I never felt she was on my side.

I could have trained to be a teacher – Bali presented me with all the opportunities but I didn't take them, preferring instead to put most of my energies into my daughter. I could have gone to church, Bali would not have minded, but instead I told myself that it would confuse Molu and I immersed myself in trying to learn about the Hindu religion and culture. In the very down times in my life, I did not have my faith to cling to as my mother had – perhaps I did this consciously. Instead, unlike my mother, I clung to my daughter and the future I was so desperate for her to have.

Put quite simply, it was one where she would have the minimum of disappointments: a secure 9–5 job and a husband who would take care of her. If I am sincere, I was desperate for her to fall in love and for it to work out, but I believed this kind of love to be fleeting.

When Bali tentatively broached the subject of an arranged introduction to me, I thought I would be completely averse to it, as I had sworn those many years ago after seeing the African dancer dance away from me that no child of mine would do the things I had had to do. But the subconscious or the conscious is a funny thing – in middle age it switches sides and defects on the promises we made in the defiance of our youth. Maybe it is the same gene that bursts through midway saying, 'Have me, I am from your father', or a combination of both. Perhaps it is as simple as the fear of moving away from the familiar – no matter how predictable the familiar may be, it seems a far better alternative than the unknown.

I was receptive, for this way we had a certain amount of control and could vet the candidates. We did not force it upon Molu, just asked her to think about it as a possibility. Bali and I began sifting through the potential applicants. There were things that were a must, such as a good, stable profession, and then there was a filtering system we had in place – those who were from abroad or those who had plans of moving away from London were instantly dismissed. Those who expressed a desire for a big family were put to the top of the pile. Bali and I worked together on these criteria and it was Bali who stumbled across Avinash Kavan.

Bali made a few inquiries and found that he was well-respected in the community. Before introducing him to Molu, Bali and I did the preliminaries and met the family. They lived in a pleasant house in a quiet suburb with nice curtains and crochet doilies for the tea to rest upon. Gobi had worked his way up from being a petrol attendant to owning the station, and his wife Laxmi had stayed at home and looked after their three daughters and their only son.

Avinash helped his father when he could but was determined to go to university. He studied law and became a successful barrister, demonstrating his tenacity and his determination. These were qualities that had been praised over and over again, hence his slightly overgrown head filled with a little pride and arrogance. I noted this and tempered it with the fact that it was something that Molu could manage well.

Laxmi handled him as if he were her prized trophy, dusting him and looking at him as if all of perfection were embodied in his 5'9" stature. A mother's prerogative, which she made much use of by stating that he had seen many girls – all had MBAs, were tall, slender and fair, but he had liked none of them.

Avinash was a handsome man and I could see how he could have had his pick of women, but there was something about his smile. Almost very pleasant, nearly symmetrical, but for the fact it cornered upwards to one side of his cheek. From all the subsequent meetings and from all the words and embraces we exchanged it was his smile that I sat uncomfortably with – it eroded the side of his mouth, giving a suppressed, cornered look, but I told myself that I was looking for things that weren't there.

He was incredibly polite and pleasant, and was able to converse on a range of topics. He appeared genuinely interested in us, had no plans to move abroad and wanted at least two children.

Molu liked him. I don't know whether this was because Bali and I had influenced her decision by talking about him non-stop, or because when she met him she felt her heart race and her hands turn sweaty – I hoped desperately that it was this but did not ask.

The animation of the wedding preparations brought new life to our home. A whirlwind of activity brought Meena, Asha, even Sasha and I closer together. It gave us something to rally around and unite against. I put all my efforts into organising the wedding with the same military precision that my father had run his household.

So when Molu came crying the day she saw Avinash Kavan with fingers caught in the locks of a curly brunette, I wanted to laugh my same laugh that made me look sick, to hold her tight and tell her I was happy for her, relieved even; that she would find the real thing if she held on and was strong enough. But my thoughts were on the plans that had to be undone and all that came out was an uncontrolled look of stern disappointment.

I know it took a lot for her to do – the day Molu came telling me she wanted to be an actress. If she had come that far with so much passion and conviction in spite of all the obstacles I had placed in front of her, she would make it – and who was I to stop her? And the day she would fall, for life is like that, I would be there to catch her: and if I wasn't, I knew now that she had the confidence to rise alone.

My heart did what it had always wanted to do. Sitting there amongst the familiarity and comfort of my friends and my nice neat home, in one statement I comprehended the power that I had to release her. 'Go and do it, be an actress,' I shouted. And then I let go, emitting the belief that I was keeping her safe from the fear and disappointment that is all part of life. I also released myself from the bitter fear and disappointment that has been my life.

Cool, refreshing, simple love, a bottled fragrance that is there every day, is how I wanted to describe my feelings for Bali. It is like this on occasions when I watch him sleeping, innocently like a child. Then I am triggered by a weakness that is perhaps my own vulnerability. I want to be kind to him but all that comes out of me is rancour.

They should have come out a long time ago, but have rotted within me – a huge ball in my throat that I am unable to swallow; feelings that I am unable to vent because the moment has been lost. They make no sense years later, so there they sit in my throat, disgruntled words finding any opportunity to escape.

I sat alone in the company of my husband with the death of my child. Another child was sent to me, and again, in his company I sat alone, loving her, educating and disciplining her, with Bali only occasionally intervening. And then alone through the rejection adolescence brings, only to find out in the midst of this that Bali was never really there in my company, and probably never even really loved me. For over thirty years I have been married to a stranger.

The news was brought to me by his cousin Raj, the one who hid behind his bushy beard at our wedding. He came to stay with us as a stopover before taking up his new career as a computer technician in America. Bali was working, Molu was at school, so I took Raj to see the sights and taste the delicacies of the hamburgers and chips he would soon encounter.

We entered into the restaurant in Piccadilly Circus and sat at the table by the window. Watching everyone go by, I listened to his conversation and theories about 'the brain drain', to which he laughed alone, adding himself to the statistic then laughing even louder. I sat and imagined how he would say 'brain drain' in a few years' time. The heavy staccato accent gone, replaced by a long drone of brain.

The waitress came over, dressed in luminous knee-high boots and with a smile that matched. She took our order, took away our menus and added that if there was anything else we needed then her name was Wendy and she would be our waitress for the afternoon. Raj was impressed and his eyes lit up like Las Vegas with 'America, here I come', which inevitably initiated a conversation about American women and the possibility of finding the right woman and settling down. He had been married but 'dievorced', as he pronounced it.

I made no comment, which prompted him to continue, saying how lucky Bali had been in finding another wife. Incomprehension filled me as I looked into his eyes as he continued. The word 'another' resounded louder and louder. How very sad it had been when he had lost his wife and their son. 'Wife', 'son', it made no sense. I repeated the word 'wife' and he said her name. Kurmilla. I had heard that name before. Bali had mentioned it years ago over something Molu did. It wasn't making any sense – Kurmilla was Molu's aunt.

Bewildered and confused, I dropped my burger and held my composure, producing a pathetic half-giggle as if I knew everything, and inclined my head, which allowed him to carry on.

He said Bali had married her and then, of course, trag-
ically 'it' had happened – and at the time Raj thought Bali
would never be able to get over it. Bali had to leave India
to forget. He went in search of a new wife who would help
him rebuild his life. And then his fortune changed when
he met me. But Raj questioned if he was able to forget it
all when he had loved her so much and had given up his
family for her, and she hers. A love like that was strong,
he added. His statements bombarded themselves and
flooded me, so that I could only manage a gasp of 'I think
we should be leaving.'

He hoped he had not offended me by bringing up what
had passed and then insisted on paying the bill. He tipped
Miss America heavily, unaware that somewhere in the
superficiality of all his conversation he had trodden deeply
on my soul.

'Have a nice day,' she beamed.

'You have a great day too,' he replied.

Why didn't I tell Bali that evening that I knew? Why did I
continue to iron those shirts and to wait for him to return
from the hospital to share meals and empty conversation?
Why didn't I ask him why he went to a big town, why he
knocked on the Chapel door, took me away from my future
and brought me to a cold place?

It was inoffensive, stable silence.

It was that day I truly understood my mother's own inertia, which up until then I could never have comprehended.
It is sometimes just too hard to scratch beneath the surface
– you may find a broken heart which is impossible to mend,
and, harder still, you may find yourself drowning inside
that broken heart.

Instead, I cut off my long black hair, putting a place
that I had not ever wanted to visit far behind. I went home
and carried on with the monotony of a twenty-year
routine that I have allowed to consume all my waking
thoughts.

With retrospect, I know it has been pointless to blame
others for not accomplishing all that I thought I could
be. Blame comes all too easily; it's easier than acknowl-
edging any kind of responsibility. All my life I have blamed
others: my mother for not taking care of me, my father
for separating me from Rodrigo, Bali for taking me away
and lying to me. Perhaps I have blamed myself – telling
myself that I was not worthy enough, not worthy of love,
of a child, not accepting that sometimes fate has other
plans that we can never be aware of. I do know that I
have lost that girl who ran so carefree and have turned
into a woman that I do not recognise, a woman that I do
not like. What I want to tell that girl is that I am sorry
– truly sorry.

* * *

It is only now, with the luxury of the missing pieces of a jumbled head, that I have come to realise that all these years we have all shared the same fear and solitude.

I can also tell you the exact time that the courage and passion that I have so longed for blew into me. It was the day I let go, let go of Molu, of my husband, let go of what people thought and what was going to happen. I just sat there alone and from somewhere amongst the quiet whispers of stillness that comes from forgiving and accepting, I let go.

Sitting here, thinking of that moment and writing about the past and the events that led to the eruption of my heart – which is no longer anchored to a person, a place, a time or fear, but is now filled with new life – I would like to save you twenty years and tell you what I have learned about hopes and dreams: if you suppress them, you pollute a clean river with fear, regret and disappointment, and that makes it very difficult to swim and find the place which is home.

I will also tell you another thing about the magic of hopes and dreams: at any point along a journey, the day you decide to take back responsibility for your actions and put your trust and faith not in fear but back in yourself, those hopes and dreams will come flooding back and the belief and the energy that charges them will take them forward to a place that is home.

I want to end by saying that sometimes in life, even if

it is just once, you have to take a risk; take everything you truly believe in, and jump. If your vision is obscured in the loudness of uncertainty, just be still and listen. And when you see the African dancer who has finally managed to escape from somewhere deep inside, follow him, follow him with fearless courage and go to wherever he may want to take you.

BALI

Umbica Naravalam is the place in South West India where I was born upside down to the Vishavan family. I didn't actually see the world until a few minutes after my feet entered. The astrologer, a highly reputable scholar, was sitting in one corner of the room accompanied by a rusty old watch, trying to get a perfectly accurate reading by calculating my exact time of arrival. He glanced at the weary midwife and she shrugged her shoulders, at which he looked dismayed and then he nailed something down on his dry palm leaves and went away to plot my life.

The astrologer, who was also the High Priest, blessed me on my twenty-eighth day. In fact, he blessed me twice, which the village washerwoman (who always attended these cere-monies) duly noted. The Priest then tied a black string around my stomach to keep away evil spirits. The washerwoman did not stay for the rest of the ceremony but ran to the commu-nal pond to tell everyone that not only had I been born upside down but, unfortunately, I had had a double blessing.

News of this splashed fast around the communal pond as the other half-dressed women hit their wet clothes against the rocks. That afternoon, by the time they had finished, news had reached all quarters that upside-down Bali would bring bad luck.

Someone should have whispered that life was hard for everyone, though I think they knew this and so focussed on those who they perceived as being even more misfortunate, and so they hit their clothes so hard against the rocks that their own plight was almost inaudible. The men would not even bother to listen to any kind of noise. Instead, they looked for other distractions far from their nagging wives. Most of them spent their days making toddies by climbing up the tallest palm trees, extracting palm juice and adding to it whatever necessary ingredients, making a substance that temporarily filled their minds with delirious happiness. Stumbling into the fields they would lie under the sun in a half-intoxicated state, wake up sober towards sundown and then return home. They slept upon whatever punishment their wives gave them and then they began again.

I really wish that another woman had run after the first washerwoman and told her that there had been a mistake. That the High Priest had got his calculations wrong and that somewhere in his sleep, his watch had stopped. My fate, which rested upon the tip of his nail and was etched neatly on the dry palm leaves, was not just incorrect by a few minutes, but by a whole day. However, like many things, it was too late. News had gone around the immensity of the village pond and was set in the stone that surrounded it. That is how the conditions of my life were set – by a High Priest whose mind was elsewhere. I was supposed to bring bad luck to those who were close to me; this is what I was told and this is what I believed.

My father died two months later, killed by his remaining buffalo who kicked him in the chest provoking a heart attack. The beast subsequently contracted a virus, possibly due to the remorse of what he had done to my father. Everyone mourned the passing of the buffalo and sprinkled both their ashes into the pond. They then blamed both incidents on 'Bad Luck Bali' and bolted their doors when I crawled into sight.

After the death of my father and his buffalo, the house fell decrepit and filled with the stench of hunger. My brothers walked for kilometres in the direction of the scent of steamed idlies or hot rice and pulli, and when I was old enough I joined them. They never let me walk with them so I trailed behind them, copying whatever they did. They would knock on people's doors and would offer to do odd errands like fetch water from wells or cut firewood. In exchange, we would all be fed, and then we would try to get something for our mother. Our mother would be waiting for us in anticipation but always had a look of disappointment when she saw what we produced. It was like this even on the days that I barely ate anything and saved up whatever food I had for her.

With aching feet I would lie in the buffalo shed and listen to the whistle of the steam train that passed at the same hour every evening. I wondered what it looked like and if it was as big as they said it was. Then I would imagine being as tall as the steam train, surrounded by people clapping. For now, though, I asked God to make paisas, annas and rupees shower from the sky so I could buy supplies that would last us a life-time: a ball for me and some marbles for my brothers, a new roof for my mother and some cows. Even if it wasn't a shower, perhaps he could extend a few drops. Dreaming that my life would not be like this forever, I would fall asleep.

The wealthiest people in our village were referred to as the Mothalalis. They owned cows and paddy fields and lots of land. Most of the villagers worked for them, as had my father before he died. They lived two kilometres away, on top of a hill that symbolised the caste to which they belonged. The family lived with their servants in a big white house with a blue roof and green doors. Beside the house was a rice mill, a lake and several cowsheds which were all surrounded by iron gates. The gates were left wide open early in the morning and just after the hour that people awoke from their afternoon sleep.

In those humid afternoons, women came for milk with

their empty aluminium pots. Engrossed in gossiping, they would lose their watchful eye that haunted those vessels and then return with most of the contents missing. Returning home and removing the lids, astounded at the scarcity of content, they would scold their husbands for not standing up to the Mothalali and curse his wife for undercutting them.

The same fate would befall the rice sacks. Intrigued and immersed in conversation, the women from the paddy fields would leave their sacks unattended. I would, however, leave the vegetable man alone; only because of the state of his sorry vegetables.

One day, a servant boy came for me. I was seven years old. The Mothalali had managed to solve the mystery of the missing milk and rice and sent for me to give me a good beating. Once I had been marched up to the house, I was made to wait on the veranda. The sun was beaming against my face, making me sweat. I kept wiping it because I didn't want the Mothalali to think that it was because I was scared of him. He eventually awoke from his sleep and came out of the door. I first saw his enormous feet in huge leather sandals. My heart pounded at the thought of him taking one of them off and beating me with it. He slowly walked towards me and glanced down at me. To my amazement, he did not take off his thick belt that held up his loongi, or his sandal, but instead asked me to be the houseboy who would help his wife. This was a smart, intelligent decision, possibly concluded by the fact that he must have seen the dignified way that I daily pressed my nose against his wrought-iron gates.

The Mothalali was a stern man who towered over me. He was as wide as a buffalo and bellowed the same way at mealtimes when his food was late or when it was cold. A superstitious man who only went out at certain times and moved in an unusual way. He would walk proudly, exposing the enormous power of his belt.

As he slept, one of the other servant boys called Shiva and myself would undo his belt a little so that when he went for his afternoon walk his loongi would become undone as he strolled, shocking the washerwomen into salacious gossip which they would feed upon for a week or two. He would bend down – at which point the washerwomen would gasp – pick up his loongi proudly, stare at them and then adjust his belt even tighter so his stomach looked as if it would burst; and he would then continue strolling.

The Mothalali stopped his afternoon promenades when he bought his car. It was black with a bright yellow roof and the first ever car that came into the village, the town, in fact the whole State of Kerala. Thousands flocked from far and wide just to be its driver. The driving certificates they came with were irrelevant as Mothalali had his own road tests and filtering system. The candidate had to endure several of his outbursts whilst seated next to him in the car, and if he survived this he would be put through to the next stage. A young weasel-type driver by the name of Pinnie was hired to take care of the car and he forbade me anywhere near it; I could not even help clean it. Despite this fact, I gained many, many friends that year by telling the village boys stories of how I rode in it, and that one day, if they gave me all their marbles, I would make sure they could ride in it too.

The car, in fact, took up most of the Mothalali's time. He would ride around the village terrorising the other villagers with the horn. Occasionally, he would stop at various points to inspect his land or shout at the workers, but no matter what, he would always be home for mealtimes. The engine would roar from behind the gates and the horn sounded continuously until Shiva or I opened them. If he didn't go out he would sit irritably, finding any excuse to pick a fight with Thampurathi, but Thampurathi never gave in to him and just ignored him and carried on with her household duties and taking care of her children.

My Thampurathi was a fair-skinned lady who seldom smiled. When she did it lit up her face and released a set of protruding teeth that looked like the instrument used to grind coconuts. At that time, my Thampurathi was the only learned woman in the village and most of the villagers went to her to settle disputes with their neighbours, to read documents that had been sent to them which they could not read, and for marital advice or to arrange marriages for their sons and daughters.

The latter two were not really her strong points. My Mothalali had married her disregarding the stern objections of the High Priest, who said that they were most definitely astrologically incompatible due to some unresolved conflict between the sun and moon and which would also affect the fate of their children. He made her his wife anyway because she came from the only family in all the neighbouring villages that could match his wealth.

Soon after the wedding they realised that they had really very little in common apart from the two daughters he had given her and the two more which were on their way. So as well as going for provisions, cleaning out the cowsheds and delivering milk, I acted as a go-between. From his bellows to her silences, I made something up and got the two of them to communicate so that everything ran as smoothly as it could. The day there was really nothing left to say came a few years later when he sold his wedding band to buy a shock absorber for his car.

I worked every day and had one afternoon off to play with the boys from the village. We would all go fishing and watch the half-naked ladies washing their clothes. We discovered how to make rubber balls by covering hay with the rubber we extracted from the rubber trees and we would throw these at them and run away. When it came close to

Vishu we would make fireworks from coconut leaves, rusty keys and phosphorus, and blow them up near the pond and then watch the ladies bounce up and down screaming. Just before dusk, I would go and see my mother for that was the time she would return from the fields.

My Thampurathi did not really give me laborious chores. She was good to me and even bought me new clothes, burning the hand-me-downs from my brothers. One day she gave me a very important assignment. I was to go into town and pick up provisions for her two new babies. It would mean that I had to walk for many kilometres and take a ride on two or three carts. She put two rupees in my hand, which I clasped tightly. Do you know the value of two rupees? I could buy a thousand balls, and one or maybe two cows.

It was evening when I set off proudly, charged with an important task. But then, after walking less than a kilometre, I suddenly heard the whistle of the steam train. It was so loud. I stood for a moment feeling the sound go through my body and contemplated what to do and then I turned back and walked in its direction. I walked for two days, tasting soda for the first time, bought from the men who sold them sitting lazily beneath the palm trees. It made me feel dizzy and funny inside. I ate sweets from stalls that I could not possibly believe had existed. There were round ones and square ones, colourfully decorated with coconut and coated with sugar. In my excitement I purchased a new shirt and a wooden spin top. Then, after two days of carrying my newly acquired goods and sleeping in sheds, I saw the town. Rickshaw noise, bustle, people, lots of loud people dressed in different colours and carrying all kinds of things. I smelled smoke, cooked food and burning firewood. Then I heard it loud and clear.

I ran in its direction and there it was, bigger, stronger and more beautiful than I could possibly have imagined. The steam train.

I watched it getting ready to leave, puffing not with exhaustion but exhilaration and anticipation of all the different passengers who would climb onboard. There were hundreds of people with their goods in either sacks or suitcases fortified with string. The noise of bustling salesmen trying to sell tea, coffee, bananas and jackfruit was immediately silenced by the train's whistle. I clapped with excitement and went to pull out my money to board the train. The ticket inspector, with his huge moustache and dressed in his khaki uniform, stared at me. I wanted to tell him that I wasn't a servant boy looking to board the train illegally. He pulled out his stick; I desperately searched inside my pockets. There were maybe one or two annas left.

I did not cry; I looked directly at the ticket inspector and told him not to worry, there had been some mistake and I would be back and then I ran off.

Very, very hungry and tired, I made my way back to the village, preparing myself for the worst beating I could receive. The crickets and the frogs were screeching in the night. It was very dark but I could see Thampurathi from a distance, sitting in her chair on the veranda, reading a book by the light of her kerosene lamp. As I drew closer, she looked up. I stood upright and did not close my eyes. She stood up from the veranda and slowly walked towards me, not taking her eyes off me. I remained silent. I did not lower my head, I held my position almost defiantly.

'Next time you run away like that, make sure you take a lot more money. There is food in the kitchen,' she added, as she turned and walked away.

I ate and went to bed guilt ridden – Thampurathi deserved better from me. That night, I made a promise that I would never steal from her or cause her to be disappointed in me again.

My status amongst the other village boys had trebled. I had a reserve of marbles, balls and spin tops, all exchanged for stories of how I had mounted the big train and gone to Trivandrum. I also managed to earn the respect of my two older brothers who would now walk alongside me.

On Wednesday evening – which was my day off – after playing with the other boys I would run down the hill and see my mother. She would be waiting for me to empty my pockets and give her any provisions that Thampurathi had given me, and then she would nod. She never smiled; she never touched me or looked me in the eye, perhaps fearing the same fate that had befallen my father. She would nod once again, indicating that I had done my duty and that it was time to leave. So in this respect, my Thampurathi was everything to me – she gave me a home and fed me, and though she never showed outward affection I knew she cared about me.

Occasionally, my brothers would come and visit me, waiting for me outside the Mothalali's house. Together the three of us would sneak our way back into the main house and torment the Mothalali's older girls. When they were asleep we would tie banana leaves together and put them through the bars of the windows that protected them. Pretending they were snakes, we would hiss so the girls would wake up. They would run screaming to their father.

They were spoiled, both Nirmilla and Kurmilla. Nirmilla was two years older than Kurmilla, who was the same age as me. Their father would consent to their every whim and they knew how to play on this. Nirmilla liked to show off like her father and was forever singing, dancing and twirling around. The buffalo would sit on the veranda and watch her perform whilst her younger sister waited for instructions from her and did whatever she wanted. The Mothalali would roar with laughter at the most unfunny recitals and Thampurathi would shake her head and get on with the chores. Whenever they received new toys from him they would unwrap the parcels and make such a noise about it so I would have to see what was happening, and then when Nirmilla knew she had caught my eye she would hold up the goods.

They barely spoke to or acknowledged me apart from the times they needed me to climb up trees or fetch things for them, but Thampurathi would scold them and not allow me to be used as their servant boy. But if I felt like it, I would do the errands they sent me to do and they would allow me to play pranks on them. In this respect there was an unspoken agreement between us.

Nirmilla once violated this. She was sitting under her favourite banana tree in her blue and white school uniform, reading her book. I went around the tree and tied her two long plaits together and ran behind the cowsheds to watch what she would do. All of a sudden I heard screams, howling and tears. The Mothalali came rushing out, bellowing at his daughter. He freed her from the situation and with outbursts of sobs she whispered, 'It was Bali, Papa, it was Bali.' I was horrified – that wasn't supposed to happen.

Enraged buffalo with salivating mouth, he undid his belt and came stampeding after me. He managed to pin me against the corner of the cowshed and with wild eyes he raised his belt and incessantly plunged the buckle, thumping it into my back. As I cowered, he continued lashing until his wife came running over from the veranda from where she was sitting and demanded that he stop. He didn't or couldn't hear her and Thampurathi placed herself between us and pushed him away from me.

I shook with pain and humiliation, made worse by the fact that I knew the two girls had witnessed the whole thing from behind the window. Thampurathi picked me up and carried me into the house, laid me on her bed and began cleaning my wounds. When she left, I crawled to the sheds where I slept and made my way to the hay, whimpering like some wounded animal.

After a few seconds, the door opened. I did not look up but lay curled on the floor. It was Kurmilla, and on seeing me like that she came and sat beside me and touched my head. I ignored her. Reeling with pain, I put my head against my arms and cried. She put another arm on my shoulder and said nothing except that she was sorry; and that was the first time I felt the gentle connection of another. That was the first time that anyone had really touched me.

The buckle brought Thampurathi and the girls closer to me. The girls would smile at me and sometimes even help me with the work I had to do. Nirmilla would leave things in my quarters such as a new slate, chalks and sweets. She no longer danced around trying to impress her father or shouted instructions at her sister but spent more time with her mother helping her younger sisters. Thampurathi decided that I was not needed the whole day, she just required me in the evenings to help mostly with the milk rounds, and so for the rest of the time she wanted to send me to school and she said that she would still pay me the same.

I remember the day clearly when she brought me my blue and white uniform, and my books and my first pair of shoes – rubber-type sandals. They were all wrapped in brown paper. I ripped open the paper with excitement as she handed them to me and stared curiously at the sandals. A huge smile beamed from her face. The buffalo said nothing when the girls told him that I was attending school with them; and despite the fact he wanted to comment, he didn't, because he knew if he said anything against the way the household was being run, he would not have been fed. So he shouted at Pinnie instead and instructed him to take him for a drive.

Every morning I went to school, walking awkwardly behind the girls as I had trouble with my new sandals. After we passed Thampurathi's gates I would take them off, carry them on my shoulders, run in front and put them back on just before I entered the classroom. Having already been established as their hero, I knew most of the children who attended the local school, so in this respect the fact that I could not read or write did not matter. Kurmilla was also in the same standard but I ignored her in the classroom.

School provided an avenue for a newfound passion about things that existed outside my village. The British were white. I saw a picture of them in my professor's textbook. They looked tall and upright in funny garments. He even said that in colour they had strange eyes and hair. Amused, I began to learn this language spoken by the British, along with learning how to read and write my own.

Taking my marks home to Thampurathi I felt very proud. They were the same or even better than Kurmilla's. Thampurathi would give me half a smile with her coconut instrument teeth and I just got on with whatever work needed to be done. It was in that way that time passed. Vishu, Onam and other festivals marked the change; monsoons came and went, leaving everything green and full of possibility. Then we learned that the British had left India, but really we felt no impact, everything continued the same.

I was in eighth standard when Mothalali announced that it was time for his first daughter, Nirmilla, to get married. She had just finished school and, much to the surprise of Thampurathi and the delight of her father, she did not want to go to college. The Mothalalis – infamous for being the village marriage-brokers – would make sure that the marriage would be an event to remember, and preparations were swiftly made as soon as Nirmilla consented to seeing prospective husbands.

Nirmilla had grown up to be very pretty and dignified in her manner. All the traces of a child once spoiled had completely vanished as she made the transition, braiding her hair, wearing a sari and stepping into adulthood. She could not have been more than sixteen but she was mature and charismatic like her mother. Nirmilla was also renowned for helping the poorer castes, and when they came for milk or to grind their rice – even if the Mothalali was there – she would make sure they got a little extra for their money. Her reputation preceded her and men came from all over Kerala in the hope of marrying her.

Mothalali would not let most of them set foot through the door. He would stare at them, and if he felt in the least bit uncomfortable, the prospective bridegroom, along with his parents, would be ushered out and sent home with the fare it had cost them to come and meet Nirmilla. Mothalali inspected those who had managed to make the second stage with such circumspection that the intensity of his stare made their steel teacups shake. Many came. Thampurathi, learning from her own mistake, said Nirmilla would be able to choose the one she liked the best, and, if they were astronomically compatible, the marriage could go ahead.

Nirmilla chose a schoolteacher who taught music and literature in a nearby town. His name was Raman and he came from a good background and had many cows. He had an affable smile and looked kind enough. Importantly, he had managed to pass all of Mothalali's tests and was also the only one who managed to look him directly in the eye.

When they sat together for the first time in the company of both families, Nirmilla smiled nervously at him but he looked at her confidently, reassuringly as if he would love and take care of her. They married and the High Priest blessed the couple, praying that they would have many children and would live happily.

The whole village came out to celebrate and fireworks and musicians were brought in from the town, and paisam was distributed from the temple to all the villagers, who had been given the day off. Thampurathi and Mothalali were very proud and the villagers all wished the young couple well as they drove off with the driver in Mothalali's car, which had been decorated with orange garlands especially for the occasion. Mothalali returned home after his frantic waving and he cried – huge, blubbering sobs.

I knew I loved her the day she touched my head and sat with me in the cowshed. It was a demonstrable tenderness – she had somehow managed to touch some part of me that was inaccessible to all others, even myself. I had never felt that kind of touch, not even from my mother. Even deep in the depths of physical pain it felt warm and comforting, like I belonged there, in that moment, with her sitting by me. I would have done anything for Kurmilla – carried her tiffin carrier to school, or her books, or just walked with her. I chose to ignore her. Not allowing space for even the smallest thought of possibility, I filled my head instead with her father's face of thunder.

But when I saw her in class or when I caught sight of her on the farm it felt like a fly was trying to escape from my stomach, and then when she smiled at me it felt as if this fly was trapped in my throat so I would be left speechless and would look away. Choke, almost. She was unaware that I would go to where she sat after she had finished her meals and clean away at her place, just inhaling her smell; or that I would watch her read out letters for those who couldn't read, watching her fingers as she held the page, the shape of her mouth as it moved and the way she tilted her head back when she laughed. She was a person who people naturally gravitated to for her laugh was infectious. I tried to remember this laugh every night before I fell asleep. And the more the uncontainable obsession grew in my head, the more I ignored her.

A little after Nirmilla's wedding, in the monsoon, Kurmilla began passing notes to me. Such insignificant things, writing about the rain, but I held on to each word, deciphering some hidden meaning. At first I did not write back, but then, as more notes were sent, I could no longer escape her. I would ponder for hours and hours, rereading every word, and then write back to her in my neatest hand, trying to show her something of myself through the way the words were put together, and then I waited anxiously for the response. Sometimes it would not be immediate but would take days: and these days of waiting were agonising. By monsoon, the notes turned into the longest letters, the letters into secret meetings, and I allowed myself to completely love her. And loving her gave me a sense of purpose; a sense of meaning to all that had gone before.

We both finished tenth standard. I won a bursary to go to Kerala State College and Kurmilla wanted to study to become a schoolteacher. It was just around this time of finishing high school that Mothalali began receiving several marriage proposals for his daughter. Thampurathi refused all of them, saying that the girl needed time to study. This was the cause of major arguments in the house as Mothalali argued that if she kept refusing such decent proposals, nobody would want to marry her. Then, if she was not married off, nobody would want the younger two daughters. But Thampurathi held firm.

The arguments went on for months until fate interceded, bringing along an elderly villager. The elder was of the same caste as the Mothalali, and this esteemed elder's son had gone to work on the tea plantations in Ceylon. Apparently he had started a plantation of his own and had amassed a fortune that tripled the Mothalali's. People flocked to his feet, coming from afar, enticed by the fragrant smell of his rupees. One day, upon returning home for his vacation, he had gone to the temple with his father and had seen Kurmilla there. He made a few inquiries and later that afternoon he was sitting on the veranda drinking tea with the Mothalali.

The buffalo looked delighted and was laughing uncontrollably. It was later that evening that the Mothalali announced he had arranged Kurmilla's marriage; a truly perfect match. It was to take place within the month. Thampurathi protested, even refusing to cook for him, but this seemed to have no effect. He said he had given his word, and his word was his honour.

Even though I knew that this was always the way it was going to be, my heart sank. I sat for hours trying to think of all the things that I could do to stop the wedding, but there was nothing. I was a nobody; I had nothing.

Kurmilla came to me that night and asked me to take her away, to marry her. I said I couldn't, I had nothing to offer her, and then there was the family to consider – think of what would happen to the twins, their father in disrepute, and to Thampurathi. Kurmilla begged me. I asked her to go back into the house; I said I did not love her and then I walked away.

That night I felt the pain and the fear of that buckle wedged in my heart, pulling at it, ripping it away, and in a state of torment and confusion I fell into a deep sleep. I saw the African dancer emerge from the hole in my heart. He crawled out, dancing to the surface. 'Take her away with you,' he whispered. 'Take her.'

So I got up, and as I had done as a child I put the snake that I had made from banana leaves through her window and tickled her feet. 'Let's go,' I whispered. She stirred to life with such energy, gathered a few belongings and came out to meet me at the back door. We held hands and walked slowly towards the iron gates.

It was nearly dawn and we had not realised that Thampurathi was up, seeing to her cows. We passed the sheds quietly and then suddenly, from nowhere, she came out. Silence. She was motionless, just staring at us both and the belongings clutched tightly in Kurmilla's hands. I wanted to say something but I couldn't.

'If you leave this house, don't ever come back. Ever,' she whispered. Thampurathi then removed the chains that she was wearing, and from her blouse she pulled out a purse filled with gold coins and placed them in my hands. With tears streaming from her eyes she kissed us both and said, 'Take care of her, my son.' We left.

The darkness in which we had left followed us to the train station. We barely spoke to each other as we both comprehended the gravity of the situation. And yes, I loved her like I could love no other woman, but betrayal, loyalty, duty and tradition weighed heavily on my conscience and took me to a sombre place. She slept with her head against my shoulder as we headed towards Trivandrum, and I looked out of the window into the dawn and wondered how we would manage and how I would provide for her.

As we got off the train we were met by rickshaw drivers, porters, fruit sellers and innkeepers, all trying desperately to make us part with our money. I looked for a friendly seller. From the crowd a young man stood out notably; he offered us good rates on a hotel and also offered to show us around the area. His name was Raj; and he also accompanied us to find a temple where Kurmilla and I could be married.

It was the 7th of November, an inauspicious occasion. Kurmilla and I were dressed in our only clothes, which had been dirtied by the rickshaws splashing through puddles. The Priest said a prayer and we exchanged some old jasmine garlands, the only ones we could find that had been untouched by the rain. I took my wife's hand and we walked around the fire and it was done. The whole thing could not have lasted more than five minutes. The wedding feast consisted of some rice and sambar on a banana leaf, which we shared with our only guest, and he took us to our hotel room and said he would return and help us find somewhere we could live.

Sitting on the rusty bed, looking up at the fan that barely managed to rotate full circle, I shook my head with disappointment. She deserved much more. Kurmilla put her arms around me and made me want to believe that it would all work out and so this is what I clung to.

We moved to our new house, which we were to share with Raj and his family. We occupied just one room. Raj managed to get me a job at the train station and I would go there every evening, working as a porter whilst attending college during the day. Kurmilla gave tuition to all the children of the neighbourhood. We barely saw each other but made time on Sunday evenings when we would do something special like go to the cinema. Almost a year passed like this, and then we had enough money along with what Thampurathi had given us for a small deposit on our own house.

The house was tiny but had a courtyard which we shared with our neighbours and where we could grow our own vegetables and keep a cow. In the evenings, when I was away working, everybody would congregate in the courtyard so at least Kurmilla wasn't on her own. Children would run around playing with the stray dogs and cats; women would wash their clothes out or be cooking.

Kurmilla befriended them all, reading letters that they were unable to read or helping their children when she had time, and though they barely had anything, what they had they shared with us. Abuchi, the old lady who lived next door, would bring us plantains she smuggled back from the fields; Nandan would give us lifts in his rickshaw; everyone helped each other in any way they could. And although our roof leaked and the walls were damp, this was not what I saw, as my wife made that house so nice with bright colours and filled it with the scent of fresh flowers and incense.

We were trying to save enough money so there would be no problems when I went to university and when the baby we were expecting arrived, but it was hard – hard watching her wear the same clothes almost every day and to pass a sari shop and not buy her anything – but I reminded myself that we had each other, and no amount of money could buy what we had.

I am not looking back with nostalgic feelings; I know that we were happy. Of course we argued, but about the petty problems of not having enough money or the intensity that comes from being apart and isolated from family, and the busyness of our lives and the days which did not allow us to see each other as much as we wanted. Despite this, I knew back then I had everything I could have ever dreamed for. It was parcelled up in an everyday routine of studying, of being with my wife, our friends and neighbours, the stability of work and the expectancy of new life.

The stench of anaesthetic and urine is what I remember of that day. The doctor mumbling some words and shaking his head, Raj gripping me, trying to pick me up from the floor. Heat and vomit pulsating from my body, and, of course, pain and anger so strong that I pulled at the hairs of my head, tearing them out. A broken glass lay on the floor in the kitchen where they said she fell, clasping at the pain in her head. Abuchi heard her screams and ran to see what had happened. They could not tell me it was pain-less or serene, for I saw her lying there in the hospital – the look that was left upon her face did not show me that. It was too late. The baby was taken out of her but he did not want to make it without his mother.

Now, I choose not to dream. I followed the African dancer, once upon a time, and he took me to a place that I never want to return to.

After the death of my wife and son I thought I would never be able to breathe again, or to put one foot in front of the other. Raj took me home and I don't remember much else after that. Weeks went by and all I could hear was the absence of her laughter and the incessant sound of water leaking into aluminium pots. I left them there to overflow and I left the flowers to rot. After a while, even the neigh-bours stopped coming, because they realised that there was nothing anyone could do or say. From morning till night I slept there in the bed she slept in, refusing to get up, not caring if they came to take away the house, not caring if it crumbled around me. I lay there trying to inhale her smell, and eventually even this left me as the dampness engulfed the house and made everything smell of death.

Inside and outside there was a vacuum that I had fallen into and beyond this there was another void and another. It was Abuchi's granddaughter who somehow managed to reach me. One evening she came dancing into the room, sat beside me and said, 'Uncle, Kurmilla auntie said it was true that when Somi went to heaven he could see me, so then Kurmilla auntie can see you too and she will be saying that you are sleeping too much. You're sleeping only.'

I could hear my wife's laughter. And those were the words I used to tunnel my way out of the place that I had found myself in.

When I was able to, I wrote Thampurathi a long letter trying to explain. I am ashamed to admit this but I did not even have the dignity to face her myself, sending Raj instead to break the news with the letter. A few months later I left our home and went to study medicine to try and cure the incurable.

Those years of studying are covered with lectures and textbooks and trying any way to scramble away from grief and solitude. There were many drunken nights in the hope that I could catch a few moments back with her, to touch her again or to feel her cold feet against my skin. In the sober mornings I would be convinced that it was not real, a cruel nightmare, and as I opened my eyes it would come back all over again. The pain did not get better. Raj was there, trying to distract me with futile games of rummy, but his friendship was not enough to take me through the acute sense of loss and sadness. I had to find a way to escape the reminders of the things she liked – the sounds and the smells – and above all to stop the screaming in my head. I didn't want to feel any more and I did everything I could to make this happen.

It was in the early sixties that I left India. I went from the rickshaw and cart to cabs and buses, from the kasavu mundu to the mini skirt, the sitar to psychedelic tunes, from red land to fertile green – England. One of my professors at university came to do some research and I was chosen to be his assistant. The contrast in cultures was so stark that it was the best thing that could have happened – there was something else to focus on.

All those weeks listening to All India Radio, trying to understand the British accent; all those hours I studied when I knew that I was the one who was picked to go to England; all were wasted when I heard British people speaking. Not like the Queen of England; it was something else. To be fair to them, they could not understand me but gave me their time, finding me an exotic curiosity. I was treated with a hospitality and courtesy that was, unfortunately, not extended by all to the many more of us who 'came off the boat' as the decades passed.

I made myself fall in love with England the first time I came. Everything so rich and green, so many ideas and concepts, such politeness. I was so fascinated by the Underground that I spent days riding aimlessly around London and then I found all those amazing monuments that I had read about as a child – Big Ben and the Queen's residence. Everything was bigger and better. There were good pavements with roads and organised traffic, gardens, parks, cinemas, and a variety of fruit and vegetables kept neatly in food stores.

At the university where I was studying and helping my professor, students invited me to parties. There I would discover music and new friends. We would dance until the morning – there was no time to be alone. And although there was no communal life as such in London, where people were out on the streets, cooking and cleaning, and despite the fact that it was quiet in comparison to the bustle and noise of Kerala, it was somehow able to fill the emptiness. It was in this way that a year passed so rapidly. It was time to go home, back to Kerala.

I dreaded going back and counted the days that I had before returning to the void. I had a conversation with my professor and asked him if it was at all possible to arrange the paperwork so that I could stay and work on transferring my qualifications and complete the last phase of my medical training in England. He said he knew a few people who might possibly be able to sponsor me and he would see what he could do. I think had he not been able to do this I would have thrown away my education and got any job in London just to stay, but a few days before I had to make this decision he came to see me one evening to say that it was possible. London was to be my new home; a new start.

The student accommodation I was living in had to be vacated as there was no longer a bursary to cover all my costs. It was really then that I came to realise how very expensive things were. Without money in those first few months, everything was so difficult, and the cold that I had not even noticed before was heightened. A feeling of homesickness and loneliness began to set in – I missed the simple things, from the errant cows wandering across the road to the smell of wood smoke. It is only now that I understand that no matter where you are you cannot escape what you are running from; it follows you everywhere, it becomes part of you. What you can do, though, is pretend it is not there. I did this by occupying every spare moment I had with work.

I managed to find work as a porter in a hospital nearby, and through my work I found a friend, a nice chap called Govinder who in turn introduced me to a little Asian community living in Bayswater. They had a bed available in their flat and I moved in with them, a group of four students and two professionals. And although all of us became friends, something was always missing.

One by one, the occupants of that flat began to get married. Mostly to girls from back home; one or two to English girls. More and more, the void was becoming apparent. One day I had a strange conversation with Govinder, one which was to change the course of events for me.

Govinder knew that I had been married before but did not delve into the details of what had happened, nor did I explain. The only thing that he really knew was that I would never return to Kerala, even if it was to find a wife. Govinder, who was from Goa, to the north of Kerala, talked to me about finding a wife from there. It was the best solution, he said, commenting that Goan women were more 'Western' and they would have no problem fitting into the British culture. Govinder would be returning to Goa shortly to see his fiancée Meena, and from there he said he would send me details of good, prospective families looking for husbands for their daughters. Reluctantly, I agreed, thinking that perhaps it was time to move on with my life.

Weeks later, a letter arrived on my doormat from a Colonel Vasco. Enclosed was a picture of his daughter, Sheila. I looked at the photograph for a long time. She was wearing a green dress, and aside from being beautiful she had a smile that conveyed so much warmth. I thought about it a lot but didn't contact him immediately and instead, thinking about the many cultural differences there would be between us, I put the photograph on my desk under some papers.

The photograph of Sheila managed to work its way out from under the pile of papers and was placed against the wall. Every morning when I woke up, I saw her there. And perhaps it was wrong of me but I imagined what she would be like and had conjured up a picture of her in my mind even before I'd met her. And when I found myself talking to this girl in the photograph, I decided it was time to do something about it.

On one cold, wintry morning, I contacted Colonel Vasco. Two days later I bought a flight ticket to Goa, hoping to marry legitimately, traditionally, and to bring my wife – with her father's consent – to England.

Sitting on the veranda of Colonel Vasco, I caught a glimpse of his daughter Sheila. I had met several women but none had touched me like Sheila did. She ran across the courtyard so full of energy and life and looked so confident, as if she could take on anything. She was slim and was beautifully fair with dark brown eyes. It was her – the woman I had imagined from the photograph. I felt something for her instantly.

I did not tell her father that I had been married before. I don't know why. I think it was just because I wanted to erase that part of my life and to begin again and maybe even to save my new wife from the insecurities of a past that was over, finished. I told Colonel Vasco that I wanted to take my new wife to England where I would finish the remaining year of my medical training. He consented, saying it would be no problem, that Sheila had always wanted to go to England – it had been her biggest dream – and if she were in agreement then he would arrange a formal meeting.

Sheila smelled of the fresh lilies she had in her hair and I remember this moment now when I pass a busy tube station and am stopped by the intense smell of lilies on a flower stall. Fresh lilies and neatly manicured long fingers that kept touching a nervous smile. Fingers that felt my hand as she gave me something to drink, laughing at the clumsiness of my own. I asked her lots of questions about herself, questions that I thought I had the answers to. She answered them and asked me just one – and that was if I liked Goa – and then I asked her if she would be my wife.

A handful of people were present at our ceremony. Raj came from Kerala and it was good to see him; it had been almost four years. Sheila's mother unfortunately took ill and could not attend, but her father stood there boldly with his pistol and sword, compensating for his wife's non-appearance, and her sister, Sasha, was also there. I could not really see my wife through her veil but I felt she was slightly nervous but happy. I took her hand, holding on tightly. Everything would be all right, and I would provide for and take care of her.

After the marriage we had to drive down to Trivandrum, as Raj had informed me that some papers releasing my old house were well overdue. I can remember that ride so well. Sheila talked non-stop with such youthful energy, and I cannot tell you the sense of optimism this gave me. But then when I left her at the hotel and went to sort out the deeds I was gripped with an intense feeling of guilt. With a desire to leave for England as soon as we could, the following day we went to the airport and took a plane.

Sheila fell silent when we landed in London. She became cold and distant, and it has been this way ever since. I know it must have been difficult for her, far from her family and friends in a country that she was not accustomed to, and with me working for most of the day, but I was doing it for us, for our security. Perhaps it was my fault; perhaps the Sheila I married was the one conjured in my head – the one who could understand my loneliness and my longing and make everything better. So in this respect, the expectation was impossible for anyone to fulfil.

Late in the evenings I would arrive from the hospital and my meals would be cooked ready, the house would be clean. But from my wife came no warmth or communication, only a sense of duty and obligation. I worked even harder, retreating from the silence that bounced around the walls of our house.

It all changed when she fell pregnant.

News of the baby was really the start of our marriage. Sheila was so happy and she found some time to love me. The guilt that I had carried about marrying another slowly abated as I felt that, finally, I had been given a second chance. With this, I made an effort to really be with my wife, to really love her without feeling a sense of remorse or betrayal. And as I loved her, she turned into the woman I believed her to be.

We would spend hours together, really getting to know each other and making plans about the future; and in those moments of intimacy I really did want to tell her about Kurmilla but I didn't want to spoil what we were building. This was hard because she revealed things about herself which must have been painful; what she was like when she was younger, the things her father had done to her. I wanted to tell her that I understood about not being loved – that my mother never acknowledged me as a son and when news reached me that she had died, I felt nothing. Instead, I told her about my brothers, how they had moved away and how we had all lost touch but it wasn't important because she was now everything to me – my family.

I found out that the silences at the beginning of our marriage were caused by her feeling cheated by me. Colonel Vasco had omitted to tell her that she was coming to London. Sitting there together on the sofa, with her head on my lap, she laughed about it when I told her that I hadn't lied to her, and said that it wasn't important any more. It didn't matter where we were as long as the three of us were together.

If you have an obsessive fear about something, do you make it happen? Maybe it was me. Maybe they were right all along – that I was born to bring bad luck. Maybe I was being paid back for taking Mothalali's child and not protecting her. What if I had spent more time with Kurmilla maybe I could have seen that she was unwell. Or was it because I began to truly love someone else?

No sadness came when they told me that our child did not cry, nor would ever cry; and, in all honesty, I was unable to feel and did not suffer the pain of losing him, nor of losing Sheila somewhere in the depths of her own emotions. I took life and I carried on.

Sheila's sister Sasha came as a welcome relief in a household suffused with tension. A lot of weekends were spent in caravan parks, extricating her from difficult situations she had managed to find her way into. Their relationship was a strange one: Sasha had so much admiration for her sister but Sheila ignored her, though she ignored a lot of people. The more Sasha was ignored, the more extreme her behaviour was.

For Sheila's fortieth birthday, Sasha insisted on organising a surprise and duly called up all our friends and relatives. I should have known when she asked them all to leave their children at home but it never even occurred to me what she was thinking of. Everyone was assembled in the dark; we could hear Sheila putting her key through the door and then a strange voice asked Sheila if she lived at the property. Sasha began to giggle. The voice then said he had a few questions to ask Sheila. As she entered, the lights were switched on and standing beside her was a policeman. The music began playing and to everyone's horror the policeman began to strip, wishing her a very happy birthday as he jiggled around her. After this incident, Sheila made Sasha move to the next street.

I wasn't even slightly angry with Sasha as I understood her need to try and get her sister's attention in any way she could. If this meant being loud and being the centre of attention, she did it. If it meant making inappropriate jokes she would bring out every one she knew and laugh uncontrollably. Perhaps she hoped that some of this laughter would infect Sheila positively and break through the wall that no one was able to penetrate, but it alienated her sister even further.

I missed Sasha, even though she did not live very far away, because with her went the unpredictability, the untimely humour and the silence returned. Perhaps it wasn't as bad as when we were first married, but it was definitely there.

I really did not intend to tell a lie. I omitted telling the whole truth and this was to protect Sheila, but I have found that one half-truth left hanging mutates. It cascades and spirals out of control and the only way I could try and contain it was by being silent. Raj forwarded a telegram from Thampurathi sent to the old house: the postman rang the bell to give it to us. Even before I had the chance to assimilate the contents, Sheila was looking over my shoulder.

NIRMILLA AND RAMAN KILLED. CHILD WITH US.

Seven words that jumped out at me to create an inconceivable mixture of sentiment, halted by one question from Sheila.

'Who are Nirmilla and Raman?'

One more lie. 'My brother and his wife.'

'Who is the child?'

I didn't even know if it was a boy or a girl. 'It is their child,' I replied, making my way to the table so I could sit down.

'I'm so sorry about your brother, Bali.'

I nodded.

'Thampurathi?' she continued.

'Nirmilla's mother – the child's grandmother.' She sat opposite me, put her hand on mine. 'Don't you see, Bali, don't you see? She wants you to go and bring the child,' she pleaded.

'No.' A flood of reasoning inundated me.

'You must, we must, it was meant to be.'

'No,' I shouted.

I never raised my voice. She looked at me, hurt, and took her hand away.

With that resolute no, silence entered our house once again and was broken approximately a year and a half later with another telegram, asking me to go and fetch the little girl.

As I landed at Trivandrum airport my stomach churned. Having taken their daughter I was back to take their grandchild. A very old Pinnie came to meet me in a dilapidated old car that barely moved. He smiled a toothless smile and held out his hand.

'The Mothalali?' I inquired.

He shook his head.

'The twins?' I asked.

He informed me that they had finally managed to get married and both were now settled somewhere in the Gulf and had their own families.

The ride to Umbica Naravalam was uncomfortably hot

and sweaty and I had such unbearable cramp in my stomach that we had to stop several times. It was the same route I had taken those many years ago after stealing from Thampurathi, the same road that I took with Kurmilla whilst going to the train station. I thought it was a journey I would never have to make again. But then life has a way of pulling you back to your roots, no matter how hard you try to escape.

As we drove past the paddy fields and into the village, my heart beat even faster. Everything seemed so much smaller. The village lake had new stones surrounding it, placed much higher than those that had been there previously.

'Several drownings,' informed Pinnie.

The temple had been painted white. One of the palm trees that sheltered it had been cut down, and in its place an enormous loudspeaker was installed to call the villagers for prayers. We passed my mother's old house which had been completely renovated and from the washing that was displayed, it looked as if a young family were living there. I hoped that they would have more luck than we had had. I thought about my brothers – where they could be and what they could be doing and overwhelmed with emotion, I wanted to turn back.

We reached the top of the hill. Pinnie sounded the horn; a little servant boy came over and opened the rusty iron gates.

The mill was no longer buzzing; it had ceased doing so a while ago. The cowsheds were numerous but there was only one cow. The banana trees were still there, standing taller and wider. Then, I saw her, sitting where she always sat. Thampurathi, rocking on her chair on the veranda, half her old size and with no teeth. The impeccable sari gone, and in its place a dull blouse, loongi and an old shawl. I bit my lip.

She stood up awkwardly and nodded and just then from behind the door came running and screaming 'Ammamma.'

A little girl came twirling along, trying to balance herself on the edge of the veranda, and then she ran over to clutch her Ammamma's loongi as she said hello to me.

'This is your uncle,' she said to the child.

I took a deep breath: before me was the image of my wife as she had been as a child. Tears welled in my eyes and I had to turn around pretending to go and get the presents from the car that I had brought for her.

I offered her the gifts.

'Molu, say thank you to your uncle,' said Thampurathi, sitting down again.

'Thank you,' she shouted as she ran over, taking them rapidly then running back to where she sat.

'Remember, Molu, I told you that Uncle was coming to take you to a nice place today?' Thampurathi said.

'Aren't you coming, Ammamma?' she screamed.

'Not today,' replied her grandmother. 'Go inside and get your doll so you can show her to Uncle.'

When Molu had gone inside, Thampurathi turned to me. She looked so frail and vulnerable.

'It's better if you do not stay; just take her and go.' Her voice quivered.

A lump formed in my throat. 'We will do our very best for her.'

'And your wife, you promise me she will love her like her own?' She was trying not to cry.

I nodded.

'Thampurathi, I am . . . I am so deeply sorry. Not a day goes by that I do not think of her.'

She was about to say something when Molu came running out with her doll.

'She's called Nirmilla, after my Amma. Ammamma says you were good friends with her.'

'Yes. I was. Very good friends,' I replied, attempting to smile.

'Molu, let's go back inside and get the rest of your things.' Thampurathi steadied herself up. I went to help her and she gestured that she would be fine and they both went back into the house.

My heart ached at the thought of Thampurathi sharing a few last minutes with her grandchild, imparting her final words. Words, no doubt, that the child would try to remember years on, that she would replay over and over again, trying to find some consolation. Tears rolled down my face. I had to stay strong; I had a child to take care of now.

A short while later, they both came out. Molu had

gotten changed and was clutching on to the red balloon I had given her. Thampurathi held her belongings and tried not to look at me as she handed them to me. I took Molu's little hand and slowly managed to get her into the car.

'Ammamma, will I come back soon?' she shouted.

Thampurathi walked over to her, kissed her and said, 'Soon, Molu, soon.' She then placed her shawl through the open window. 'You might need this, my little one, in case you get cold.'

And then she turned to me and said, 'Take care of her, my son, take care.'

The memories of the journey and how we managed to make our way home are best left forgotten. I can only say that I tried to do my best to calm her – to explain – but Molu just cried and cried until she fell asleep.

We were met at the door by Sheila, and Molu stared at her completely bewildered and then cried. Cried every day for a long time after that. Her tears eventually turned to anger and she said and did a lot of hurtful things. Things we had no answers for or no way to rationalise. Sheila took care of it and despite a tempestuous relationship, anybody could see that they loved each other, clinging on to each other so desperately that there was no room for another. I worked to give them the things they needed.

There were certain things Molu did – such as the way she danced and sang – that reminded me of her mother; and mannerisms, like the way she tilted her head and laughed, that reminded me of Kurmilla. When she spoke in Malayalam, sometimes I heard those childhood voices and the memories came flooding back, and I relived them with such fondness. I did not remain distant because these memories were painful; I think it was because I feared being too close to her, too connected, in case I lost her too. Everything I touched, I spoiled.

It's easy for me to talk about morose death, clinical white infused with the smell of anaesthetic, the relatives' room, the explanation as to the cause of death, my sincere condolences with no place for sentimentality, but yet I am struggling to find something to tell you about the three of us. I do not recollect the colour of Molu's school uniform, the subjects she enjoyed, her favourite food or who produced the sound of that constant music.

Even at weekends we were not really together. Families with problems all buffered by each other, trips out, dinners in. Then all of a sudden I am confronted with the face of a fully grown Nirmilla, who stands before me calling me Papa, and all I can think of is, where have the years gone, and have I done my duty? Have I kept my promise to Thampurathi? Will Molu be taken care of and be settled when we are no longer here? Some of you may laugh, but this is what I am thinking when the face appears before me.

Jeans and T-shirt, she speaks to me in an English accent with no trace of where she is from. I panic. Does she remember anything about India? Does she even care? Will she ever go back and then come and tell us how everything is so dirty, unhygienic and strange? The tradition and culture that runs through her – who will understand it?

Somewhere between notions of love with a happily ever after and practical, grounded stability that brings no real ups and downs there is an in between, and I found him. Avinash came from a good family, was born in London and was a lawyer in the city. They seemed a good match so I introduced them.

A few months after meeting her, he came to me asking if he could marry her. I cannot tell you how delighted we were. They were due to get married the following summer, and then three months before the wedding both Sheila and Molu told me it was cancelled and then Molu told me she was moving out and going to study to become an actress. I looked at Sheila, waiting for her to resolve the matter but she didn't.

I was very upset; Molu was throwing away a good education, a job for no stability, for a profession that was notoriously difficult. Sheila put up no resistance and left our daughter to go and do whatever she wanted. So she did, with an 'I'll be fine, Papa. You'll see I'll be fine.' Two days after that, Sheila left me. I read the note left on the telephone and went back to work the following day.

Every day I see patients with haemorrhages. Some do not make it; some go home to recover. This morning, a young man of twenty-five came in with his pregnant wife. Desperation on his face, he shook my shoulders and begged me: 'She has to make it, Doctor, she has to – it's our first child.' As one of the nurses led him away, his wife stopped breathing and went quietly.

I walked into the relatives' room, shook my head. Then, uncontrollable grief seized him like I had seen it on no other. He fell to the floor, screaming as he pulled at his hair. I asked the nurse to leave. I held out my hand and went to touch his head and there it entered me so peacefully, the ability to feel – compassion. I sat by his side, held him and felt his pain.

It has been such a difficult day, and in the patio of our garden I am sitting looking at everything that is so green. Green all around me. It has been three weeks since Sheila left and I miss her, really miss her. Everything is so silent – no pots thrown in temper, no music or ringing phone or smells of cooking. I miss her silence.

I have a postcard of a beach in Goa with the words 'I am okay'. It is the first real news of her that I have, and it came about a week ago. The postcard is sitting here in front of me, looking at everything that is so green, green like the dress on the photograph of Sheila that once sat in front of me all those years ago. But this time there is no expectation. I have come to acknowledge my reality. I read a book recently about a woman who was left widowed. Sitting by the coffin of her dead husband, with painted fingernails, she whispers, 'Now my life begins.' So is this how it all ends?

Do you think what you fear most is what you attract? I am looking directly at the face of loneliness, loneliness imbued with all the connotations of rejection. I see it so clearly, though the strangest thing is that I think it has been with me all these years. And you know, now that I am finally confronted with its ugly face, it is not so bad.

What I have learned is that the older one gets, the more confusing it all appears, so make use of the clarity of youth which is sent with so much energy. Maybe I will also say that whatever happens to you in your life, try not to close your heart. If it is at all possible, leave just a little space so that this space can grow bigger. What happens with a closed heart is that, no matter what is sent to fill it, it will still remain empty. I will leave you with that as I am really very tired, tired of being afraid, tired of worrying about what may or may not happen, tired of thinking.

'Go follow her, Bali – tell her, dare to love, to be hurt. Come, follow me.'

It is only the second time that I have seen him. He danced in front of my eyes and ran away.

I sat there for a while longer and then I went to get my suitcase. As I emptied its contents, I pulled out a photograph. It was of a young woman in a green chiffon dress who held much hope and expectation in her eyes.

'Forgive me,' I whispered to her.

It was time to go and bring my wife home.

Author's Note

On a cold December day in 1999, I caught a fleeting glimpse of the African dancer, jumping out of a window and asking me to follow him. He held my dream of being a writer in his hands.

Fearing insanity, I resisted the call at first and went to work, continuing to write in stolen moments of my tube journey. And then one day shortly after seeing the dancer, feeling that there must be more to it, I left my job and decided to go wherever he wanted to take me.

The journey for me has at times seemed impossible and the moments when I doubted, for there have been many, I suspended my disbelief and continued, believing that somehow it would all come together.

Gypsy Masala is a product of that dream. Little did I realise back then what I would have to go through to get this book out because maybe if I had, I would have gone straight back to work.

After receiving several rejections from publishers, I invested everything I had and decided to self-publish *Gypsy Masala*. Not having enough money for publicity, I created an alter ego and shamelessly began to hype my book myself. It sold over 2,000 copies in just one store and as everything began coming together (publicity and demand) something happened to stop me in my tracks. I watched as three years' work evaporated into nothing.

In debt and exhausted, I went away and took stock. Realising that the most important thing was to let go of the outcome, I began my second novel, *100 Shades of White*. Looking back now, I could not have plotted what was to follow.

100 Shades of White was sold as part of a three-book deal to HarperCollins and has been bought by the BBC for a television adaptation. A reissue of *Gypsy Masala* was included in this deal and has been published alongside my third book, *Beyond Indigo*. *Beyond Indigo* charts the crazy journey of a woman with nothing except a seemingly impossible dream.

Out of all of this, I have come to realise that when things don't work out the way you want them to, there is something better around the corner. And yes, I still maintain that dreams come true . . . if you want them to.

Thank you for following the African dancer and me this far.

May 2004

Read on for an exclusive extract from Preethi Nair's new novel, *Beyond Indigo*, available now.

2nd December 1999

I know now that hurling a saffron-stained coconut over London Bridge at six-thirty in the morning should have set some alarm bells off. The tramp peered up at me from his cardboard box as if to say that I would be joining him very soon. But the Guru had said that it would remove the stagnation from my life, me being represented by a hairy coconut and the water representing flow. The Thames did not glisten at me. Well, it couldn't really as it was pitch black and probably frozen, but I believed it was glistening, shimmering even, and leading me to better things.

Looking back, the only bit the Guru got right was the symbolism. Brown woman thrown further into murky waters.

* * *

I had met this Guru the previous day. I'd like to say that I met him at the foothills of the Himalayas or somewhere exotic but I bumped into him outside Pound Savers on Croydon High Street. It was one of those really cold December days when everything comes at you from all directions; the wind, the rain, puddle-slush, the odd hailstone, and anything else nature can find to throw at you.

It had been a really hard day at work and almost unbearable to get through: my best friend, Kirelli, had died exactly a year earlier. Sorting out the contract of some egotistical artist and checking the provenance of a painting for a client seemed irrelevant, so I told my boss that I had a headache and was leaving early.

'Two aspirins will clear it,' he said.

'Right, I'll get some on my way home,' I replied, with absolutely no intention of stopping off at the chemist's. I was good at pretending; it had become second nature to me because of the distinct worlds I lived in.

Having said that, there were certain parallels between the art world and the Indian subcontinent ensconced within our semi: both worlds were seemingly very secure with an undercurrent of unspoken rules and codes of conduct that were made and manipulated by a dominant few. One set fixed the price of art and the other fixed up marriages. The main difference was that the ones in the art world didn't have centre-parted hair and weren't dressed in saris, grey woolly socks and sandals.

The only way I was able to make the cultural crossover from the Hindi songs wailing from the semi to the classical music played subtly at the reception area in the law firm where I worked as an artist's representative was by pretending. Pretending to be someone I wasn't.

'Nina, Boo Williams is coming in tomorrow,' my boss reiterated before I left. This was his coded way of saying, 'Make sure you pull yourself together by the morning.'

Boo Williams was one of the artists we represented at the firm. Her sculpture of Venus de Milo made from dried fruit and vegetables had failed to win the Turner Prize so she would be needing much consolation and bullshit from me in the morning. Forget the sickie, forget grief; Boo and her heap of fruit and vegetables needed me more.

'Right, see you tomorrow then,' I muttered, grabbing my coat.

On the way back home there were no commuters hurling themselves onto the tube. The carriages were almost empty and I was relieved, because if I had had a group of wet strangers pushing against me, vying for space, that would have just about done it. I sat opposite an old lady with wispy white hair. She had the kind of eyes that made me want to tell her that my best friend had died in my arms at exactly this time – two-thirty, a year ago – and that since then I had been lost, truly lost. The old lady smiled at me and a lump began to form in my throat. I got up, moved seats and sat down beside a soggy copy of the *Guardian*. The page it was turned to showed the Turner Prize winner, Maximus Karlhein, trying desperately to pose seriously. He was standing next to one of his pieces exhibited at the Tate – an old wardrobe stuffed with his worldly possessions.

I pushed the paper away feeling exhausted. It was all nonsense; people posing in front of wardrobes, passing it off as art and making headlines. Where was the feeling? The passion? And that crap – that the relationship with his wardrobe was imbued on his soul and that he had no option but to express it – which PR person had thought of that line? Art was supposed to be passionate and full of emotion, not contrived, not like an Emperor's-new-clothes scenario where a group of influential people said that the work was good and therefore people believed it was. What had happened to art? Paintings done by artists who didn't even care if they weren't known, not some hyped artist giving a convoluted explanation behind a pile of dried fruit or a heap of junk. A year on, and despite promising that I would be true to myself after Ki's death, I still participated in the circus.

Tomorrow, no doubt I would have to console Boo. What kind of name was that anyway? Knock, knock, who's there? Boo. Boo who? Don't worry, love, your apricots didn't win the Turner Prize this year but you can sell them for at least five grand. That's what I would want to say, but what I would probably say was, 'Ms Williams, Boo, it's an injustice, I just can't see how you didn't win. Your concept, the use of colour is simply . . . simply inspirational.'

Was that what happened to you in life? You started off with such high hopes and ideals and then got sucked into all the bullshit and you pretended that that was reality. No, I didn't think that was the case with me – I knew deep down that life was too short to be doing anything other than what I really wanted to do; Ki had shown me that. But that wasn't the problem – there were the occupants living in the semi to consider. I had a duty to make sure that they were happy, and keeping my job as a lawyer was fundamental to their all-important list system.

Mum and Dad's short list was devoid of any kind of love or passion. Thinking about it, the Turner Prize short list and my parents' own were not that dissimilar: although the criteria were seemingly clear and transparent, the subject produced was, at times, truly baffling. In their case, the subject was a man and the objective of the list was to find me a husband. Like the art world, much went on behind the scenes that nobody really knew about. Favours were exchanged, backs were scratched and tactics employed so that the prospective candidate was over-hyped to an influential few in order to persuade them that he was the right man for the job.

The long list was drawn up by a group of well-connected elderly women in the community, whose demure presence betrayed what they were really capable of. The criteria that had been set to filter the candidates were that they had to come from a good family background, be well educated and have lots of money. One of my mum's roles was to whittle down the long list, but her primary task was to set the PR machinery in motion; to cover up any negatives, then to promote and hype the candidates and make sure they were shown to me in a favourable light. This week she had managed to get the list down to three potentials whose vital statistics were presented in the form of handwritten CVs. There was a doctor, another lawyer and an accountant left on the dining-room table for me to look at. The hot favourite (who had been put to the top of the pile) was the accountant, because he had his own property: 'Beta, this candidate was imbued on my soul.' She wouldn't use those words exactly, she would just draw my attention to his flat. So, although it was seemingly my decision to choose one, go on a few dates with him and agree to marriage, the system was clearly rigged.

However, the panel had overlooked one very important thing: an outsider was trying to infiltrate the system. A man of whom they had no knowledge had just asked me to marry him. The judges were going to have a problem. At best there would be an uproar: my dad would pretend to go into heart failure and my mum would do her wailing and beating on the chest routine. At worst I would suffer the same fate as my sister, who had run off with her boyfriend and who they had not spoken to since.

I didn't know what to say to Jean Michel when he asked me to marry him. It wasn't a question of not loving him enough; it was a question of making a decision and then facing all of the consequences, and I was too tired for all of that. So for a while I hadn't been making any decisions; not even daring to venture slightly outside my routine. There was a certain sense of safety in catching the tube to work, dealing with clients, going back home to Mum and Dad and seeing the CVs on the table.

I hadn't been thinking about anything too deeply except on days like that when I had been forced to. I mean, I knew Ki was dead, I had watched her disintegrate before me and then be scattered into the wind, but for me she was still there in some kind of shape or form. She had to be. Pretending that she was still there, looking out for me, was the only thing that had helped me hold it together, because otherwise . . . otherwise, everything was pointless.

Her death was senseless. Good people weren't supposed to die young. I had bargained hard with God and promised to do all sorts of things if He let her live, and although He didn't listen I held steadfast in my belief. It was the only thing that I could really cling to. I don't know how best to describe what this *belief* was, but it's the feeling that someone out there is listening and responding; that there's a universal conversation going on where forces of nature conspire to look after you and give you strength. Occasionally you'd get a glimpse of the workings behind the scenes and these were termed by others as coincidences or luck. And then there were signs. Signs were things like accidentally finding a twenty-pound note when you most needed it; a song on the radio that comes from nowhere and that speaks to you directly; words or people that find their way to you at just the right time. Ki promised she would send me a sign. A year had passed and she hadn't. Or maybe she had and I'd missed it. I had become far too busy to see any signs.

I got off the Underground and waited for the train that would take me home.

* * *

The High Street looked tired and depressed, like it too had had enough of being battered by the rain. Among all the greyness, the windswept umbrellas and the shoppers scurrying home, I suddenly spotted colour, a vibrant bright orange. I walked in its direction to take a closer look. It was a Guru, standing calmly in the rain amid a flurry of activity. I stopped momentarily, thinking that the scene would have made a good painting, and stared at the strangeness of his presence. He was wearing a long, orange robe over some blue flarey trousers and over his robe he had a blue body-warmer. As they walked past, school children were pointing and laughing at the enormous red stain across his forehead. The red stain did not strike me as much as the open-toed sandals on his feet. It was freezing, and as I was thinking that he must be in desperate need of some socks, someone called out to me.

'Nina, Nina,' shouted the man as he came out of Pound Savers, clutching his bag. He knew my dad, I had met him a couple of times but I couldn't remember his name.

'Hello Uncle,' I said, thankful that calling obscure friends of your parents 'Uncle' is an Indian thing. Any random person that you've only met once in your life has to be bestowed with this title. 'How are you?' I asked politely.

'Just buying the socks for his Holiness,' he said,

looking at the Guru, 'he's finding the weather here a little colder than Mumbai. Guru Anuraj, this is Nina Savani. Nina, this is his Holiness, Guru Anuraj.'

The Guru put his hands together in a prayer pose. If I was a well-mannered Indian girl, such an introduction and the use of the word 'Holiness' would be my cue to bow down in the middle of Croydon High Street and touch his 'Holiness's' icy feet, but instead I just smiled and nodded.

The Guru held out his hand. I thought he was angling for a handshake so I gave him mine. He took it, turned it palm up and muttered, 'Been through much heartache. Don't worry, it's nearly over.'

'He's very good, you know. For years Auntie was becoming unable to have baby and now we are expecting our child,' acquaintance man interrupted eagerly. 'Guru Anuraj was responsible for sending child,' he beamed.

The Guru's warm smile spun out like a safety net as he told me my life would improve greatly in two weeks. Although his smile was warm I chose to ignore the fact that it was full of chipped and blackened teeth. If I had paid attention to his dental hygiene it could have given me some indication towards his character and all that was to follow without having to take his palm – 'cleanliness being next to godliness' and all that – but as he made promises of being able to remove the stagnant energy which was the cause of much maligned obstacles, I chose not to see the warning signs. I wanted him to tell me more but the Guru had his socks to put on. He'd also spotted the grocer roasting chestnuts, and indicated to acquaintance man that he might like some.

Before he left, he delved inside his robe and handed me a leaflet. 'Call me,' he said, staring intently into my eyes.

'You must call him, his Holiness only gives out his number to the very special people,' added acquaintance man. I took the leaflet and said goodbye to them both.

When I got home, Hindi music was blasting from the television set and both my parents were doing their normal activities. My mum was in the kitchen making rotis and my dad was in the sitting room, with a glass of whisky in one hand, newspaper in the other, looking like an Indian version of Father Christmas with his red shirt, white beard and big belly. He was the only person who was not engulfed by the enormous Land of Leather sofa.

'Good day, Nina?' he asked, turning back to his newspaper.

'It was really crap. Crap day, crap client, just awful.'

'Good, good,' he replied. My dad had very selective hearing and only chose to hear the words he liked or words that were of some threat to him. 'Home early, no?'

'We were all made redundant.'

He put his glass down, threw his newspaper to the floor and looked at me. Redundancy was his worst nightmare. I had to be a lawyer; years of both time and money were invested in this and it was pivotal to the list system (the spin on candidates worked both ways so I too was lying on someone's dining-room table). That was what he sold me on, the fact that I was a lawyer working for a reputable firm, and also that I was tall and quite fair-skinned, but he omitted the fact that I had one humungous scar down my left arm and that I couldn't really cook.

By my parents' standards, twenty-seven was far too late to be getting married, and my mum was truly baffled by it, saying to my father that I was one of the prettiest girls on the circuit and there was a queue of men waiting to marry me. But I had managed to fend them off so far by telling them that things were changing and men were looking for women who were settled in their careers; it wasn't like the olden days when they just wanted to know your height, complexion, and if you had long hair down to your back. It was, however, getting to a stage where this argument was wearing thin. As my dad said, at this rate I would be heading towards retirement: hence more and more weekly CVs.

'What?' he shouted.

'I said I had a headache.'

'I thought you said redundant.'

'No, just a headache.'

'Thank Bhagavan,' he sighed, glancing up to one of the many incarnated god statues.

My mum came out of the kitchen, rolling pin in one hand. 'What headache, beta? It's because you are not eating properly.'

'I think I'll just go to bed, I'll be fine, Ma.'

'Not eating with us?' she asked, looking over at the dining-room table and fixing her gaze on it. 'Rajan Mehta. He's thirty-one, an accountant. He's got his own flat in Victoria . . .'

My heart sank. I turned my back and began walking up the stairs as she shouted, '. . . three bedrooms and two bathrooms.'

I couldn't put off the inevitable. I had to tell them about Jean Michel, and tell them soon. He was away on a business trip in New York and as soon as he got back we had to sort something out. I picked up the phone to call him and put it down again; he was having back-to-back meetings so it probably wasn't the best time to call. I flicked through my address book to see who else I could phone. I had friends, of course, but nobody I could open up to. Since Ki's death I had kept all my other friendships on a superficial basis: nobody knew what was really going on inside my head as I refused to go through that kind of closeness again only for it to be snatched away. I flicked through the pages once more. No, there was no one, no one who had an inkling that anything was wrong. Anyway, where would I start? The fact that I did not allow myself to cry, that I was desperately missing Ki, that I hated going into work, or that I didn't know whether to marry Jean Michel?

Suddenly, a thought occurred to me.

'Did you send that Guru for me, Ki? Is that what you meant when you said you'd speak to me? Was he a sign?'

I pulled out the leaflet and read: 'Guru Anuraj, Psychic Healer, Spiritual Counsellor and Friend.'

I dialled the number. He gave me an appointment to come and see him the very next morning. I had a shower and went to bed.

It was five-thirty in the morning when I drove to the address he had given me. I didn't want to tell my parents that I was going to see the Guru as it would have sent my mother's thoughts propelling into all kinds of directions and that was dangerous. So when she spotted me up and about very early in the morning I told her I was driving up to Leeds for a client meeting; the lie, believe me, was for her own protection.

I know it was an odd time but my mum always said that, supposedly, between four and seven in the morning are when prayers are most likely to be receptive – that's when she annoyed all the neighbours with her howling and chanting.

'Kavitha, why you can't you learn to sing like the Cilla Black?' my dad would ask her.

'I *am* singing.'

'This is not the singing, see, neighbours have written letters doing complaining,' my dad said, producing letters that contained handwriting which appeared remarkably similar to that of his own.

'This is all for Nina, so she will find a good man, coming from a good family,' my mother replied.

'No, only man who comes will be police.'

But she continued unabated by threats of the council charging her with noise pollution. Because, for her, if it produced the desired result it would all have been worth it.

When I arrived I knocked on the door as instructed. A short man opened it and took me to the dining room where he asked me to take a seat. He said that the Guru was with someone and would see me shortly. I was nervous and excited; seeing the Guru was the first positive step I had taken in a long while. Admittedly, I was also feeling slightly apprehensive, not about being in a stranger's house but about what the Guru might say, so

I focussed on the decoration in the dining room and, like Lloyd Grossman, studied the clues and imagined what sort of family lived there. Half an hour later the man came back and led me to another room. I knocked on the door and went in.

Warm jasmine incense and soft music and candles filled the room, and on pieces of colourful silk stood statues of gods in all different sizes. The Guru acknowledged me by nodding his head and asked me to remove my shoes and take a seat opposite him on the floor. I did so nervously.

'Date of birth?' the Guru asked swiftly.

'Fourth of September, 1972.'

He proceeded to draw boxes, do calculations, and then, like a bingo caller, he reeled off some numbers which, he said, were the key events that had marked my life: aged six, an accident with the element of fire which had left deep scarring. I looked at my left arm; it was well covered, how could he have known that? He continued: aged eighteen, a romantic liaison which did not end in marriage. At this point he raised his eyebrow. Aged twenty-five, another. I saw how this could look bad to a holy Guru who believed in traditional values and the sanctity of just one arranged marriage so I avoided eye contact.

'A Western man?' he questioned.

I nodded.

He shook his head. 'It is being serious?' he asked.

I nodded again.

'Parents knowing?'

I shook my head.

'Parents not arranging anything?'

Parents were very busy arranging things. Last week the hot favourite was a twenty-nine-year-old investment banker, this week it was thirty-one-year-old, five degrees accountant Raj, the letters behind his name rolling off the page.

The Guru stopped at age twenty-six, with the death of my best friend.

'It will all change,' he promised. I fought back the tears and then he touched the palms of my hands and they began to tingle, a warm glow that made his words feel safe.

'Stagnant life now, unable to move forward, unable to take decision. See this,' he said, nodding at my palms, 'this is now flow but too much negativity in body for flow. Let it go. Let it all go.' And that's how the whole coconut-over-bridge routine came about.

It sounds bizarre now but he performed a ceremony that morning, asking permission from the gods to be able to treat me. The coconut he used in the ceremony was meant to represent me and he stained it with saffron. He did the same with my forehead so that the coconut and I were united. The river was supposed to represent new life. After mumbling a prayer, the Guru asked me to return after I'd thrown my coconut self off the bridge. I could have chosen anywhere where there was water, even the canal near where we lived, but I didn't want the coconut to sink to the bottom and find a rusty bicycle, a portent of doom if ever there was one, so I chose London Bridge.

'There will be a big change in you, Nina,' he said as I left, coconut in hand. 'Come and see me later this evening.'

After I hurled the coconut off the bridge I felt immensely relieved. I wiped the stain off my forehead and went to work, ready to caress Boo Williams' ego. I got to work only to be told that Boo was too upset to get out of bed and would be in the following day instead. Still, I was unperturbed.

Richard, one of my colleagues, commented on how well I was looking.

'I'm getting engaged,' I replied.

When the coconut had left my hands all my decisions seemed so clear. I wanted to phone Jean Michel right away to tell him that I was going to marry him. I started to dial his mobile number but decided to wait for him to come back from his trip the next day and tell him in person. Everything that day at work was effortless. I knew I wouldn't have to be there for long: once Jean and I were married I could think about other options. And my mum and dad? What would I do with them? If I looked at things optimistically, Jean could charm my mother – he could charm anyone, he was incredibly charismatic – and my mum, in turn, could work on my dad. Together we could make him come around.

Jean called me later that afternoon and I had to stop myself from blurting it all out.

'I can't wait to see you, ma chérie.'

'Me too. When you're back it's all going to change. I love you, Jean.'

All I had to do was wait one more day and all the pretence could stop.

The Guru had given me the energy to make all obstacles appear surmountable and later that evening I returned to thank him for what he had done. He prescribed one more session for the following day, just to make sure I would keep on track. How I wish I had stopped there.

The next morning the Guru's door was slightly ajar so I knocked on it and walked in. He had his back to me and was lighting his candles, humming away and swaying to Sting's 'Englishman in New York', which was playing loudly. It got to the alien bit when the Guru turned around. He looked startled when he saw me and immediately stopped the tape recorder, saying that he was sampling the music that was corrupting the youth of today, and promptly changed the cassette to a whinging sitar.

'Sting is not a corrupting force,' I said. 'In fact, he's against deforestation.'

The Guru glared at me when I said deforestation like he didn't know what the word meant, but now I think about that look – eyes narrowing, brows furrowed – it was probably more that he remembered he had a job to do.

He signalled for me to sit on the floor and held my hands. They tingled with warmth again as he whispered kind words and then he began humming and chanting. Then the Guru asked me to lie down and he proceeded to touch me, moving slowly from my hands to other parts of my body, my neck, my feet; incantations and gods' names being chanted all the while as he healed the negativity that shrouded me, asking me to let it go. As he unbuttoned my clothes and took off my top, his breath became rhythmic, his chanting louder, his beads pressed against my chest. I closed my eyes, wanting to believe that I was lost between the gods' names and that none of this was really happening. It couldn't happen; a holy man wouldn't do this, he couldn't do this, this wasn't supposed to happen. His beard brushed against my skin, his fingers circled my mouth, I pretended that my trousers had not come down.

I have often asked myself why I didn't get out of there sooner and how I had got myself into such a position. I didn't want to believe what was really going on, because if I did, nothing whatsoever would make any sense – and the only thing at that point in time that I had left to hang on to was my belief. I didn't want to believe what his dry, filthy hands were doing because I would have had to concede that whoever was responsible for sending me signs had sent this Guru, who was into an altogether different kind of spiritual feeling. Nobody could be that cruel.

As he placed his salivating mouth on my lips and pulled up his robe, I smelled him, and it was this that made something inside of me snap. He smelled of coffee. I kicked him, pushed him off me and managed to get out from under him before he used his magic wand.

'No,' I shouted.

'You're cursed,' he screamed as I ran out of the door. 'Cursed, and I will make sure of it.'

* * *

How I had sunk to such depths still remains a mystery but, essentially, that is where my journey began. I was confused and desperate, feeling wholly inadequate, riddled with self-doubt and dirty. I wanted to call Jean Michel and tell him but he would kill the Guru. So I tried to block it from my mind and pretend that nothing had happened.

The train I was on stopped. Some old man with the same rotten teeth as the Guru got on. It's funny how that happens; reminders of the things you are trying most to forget. He smiled at me and I felt physically sick. My hands began to shake. 'It didn't happen,' I kept saying to myself. 'It's all in the mind, it didn't happen,' and I reached into my handbag to get a mint. While I was fishing for it I found an envelope that was marked urgent.

It was a contract that I had looked over for a client, and which had been sitting in my handbag for the last two days. I had promised to send it back the next day and had completely forgotten. But today it was all going to change. I had to hold it together.

'All change here,' announced the driver. Although running late I was determined to buy a stamp, find a postbox, and personally post this letter. Posting it myself would be symbolic of my commitment to getting my life back on track. But, wouldn't you know, there wasn't a postbox in sight.

'You're cursed,' I kept hearing, and the more I heard it, the more adamant I became that I would find a post-box and put everything behind me.

My boss, Simon, was slightly concerned when I arrived late. I was *never* late.

'Is everything all right, Nina?'

'Fine, just fine,' I said, making my way to my desk.

I turned on the computer and looked out of the window. The buildings were grey and dreary and set against a grey winter sky. So many times I had sat look-ing out of this window, imagining the sky to be orange, wishing that I could soak up the rays of an orange sky, fly out of the window and have the courage to do some-thing else, something that gave me meaning.

I had been working at Whitter and Lawson for the last three and a half years, representing all kinds of artists but mostly those who had issues over copyright or needed contractual agreements with galleries drawn up. I read somewhere that people work on the periph-ery of what they really want to do so that they don't have to cope with rejection. So, someone who harboured desires to be a racing-car driver would be a mechanic on a racetrack but not actually drive the car. It was like this for me in a sense: I'd always wanted to be a painter and so I worked with artists. But my job wasn't really about art, it was about making money, dealing with boosting egos. Feeling increasingly cynical and secretly thinking that I could do much better. But I couldn't – it wasn't really rejection I feared, it was disappointing my father and sabotaging his investment in the *Encyclopaedia Britannica*.

I'd known I wanted to be a painter since the age of six. My brain had always had difficulty engaging with my mouth and I was unable to fully articulate any emotion except on paper. So anything I felt, I produced in a swirl of finger-painted colours that nobody could quite manage to understand. When I found out that my sister wasn't coming back I did more of the same. My parents didn't hang the pictures on the fridge door with a magnet – they didn't know that that is what you were supposed to do with the nonsensical pictures that your children produced. They didn't even lie and tell me how good they were. Instead, the pictures were folded up and binned while my father would sit with me and read me bits from the *Encyclopaedia Britannica*, extracts that even he didn't understand. He was preparing me for a career in law, or 'love' as he mispronounced it.

His career choice for me was not based on any long-standing family tradition. He was a bus driver and I think he just wanted to give me the best possible start, and make sure I would not have to face the instability that he had suffered. That's why when the encyclopaedia man came round when I was young and sensed the aspirations my father had for me, he blatantly incorporated me into his sales pitch by saying that the books would set me on course for a high-flying career. My dad bought the whole set, which he could clearly not afford, taking on extra jobs like mending television sets so he could buy the entire set and receive the latest volume, year after year.

At sixteen, when I expressed a desire to go to art college he went ballistic and didn't speak to me for weeks. When he did it was to say, 'Nina, I have not sacrificed the life so you can do the hobby, the lawyer is a good profession. Not that I am pressurising you, not that I came to the England to give you the good education and work every hour and make sacrifices.'

Put that way I could clearly see his point. So I did an art A level without him knowing about it – just in case, by some miracle, he changed his mind. He didn't and so I went to university to study law.

Whitter and Lawson was where I did my training, and I worked incredibly hard so that they would give me a job after I had finished; at least that way I could be around artists and connect with their world. Everyone around me said it was impossible, there were hardly any Indian lawyers representing artists and it was a place where contacts mattered. People said that I would need a miracle to be taken on by the firm but I busted my gut and worked every single hour I could, going out of my way to prove everyone wrong.

I remember making promises that I would do a whole series of things if I got the job, like give away ten per cent of my future earnings to charity and buy a *Big Issue* weekly. To whom these promises were made I couldn't really tell you; maybe just to myself. So I should have known that the first visible sign of wanting out was crossing the road, making out like I hadn't seen the *Big Issue* man when he was blatantly waving at me. But I pretended, pretended that I was lucky to have a job and make lots of money and be in that world. My dad always said this was what life was about – working hard, being disciplined, making money, surviving in a 'dog eating the cat' world. But then my best friend Ki died and none of that made sense any more. An uneasiness began to set in.

Felicity, the PA, called me to say that Boo Williams was waiting for me in reception.

Ki disintegrated rapidly at twenty-five. She had felt a lump in her leg while she was away travelling but decided it was nothing. By the time she came back it had spread throughout her whole body. There was nothing anyone could do. I pretended it would be fine; didn't even see the head scarf and the dribbling mouth and the weight loss. She whispered lots of things to me and I made a whole heap of promises to her. I'm not sure exactly what I said, I wasn't really there so couldn't remember any of it. Not until that moment, the moment I sat at my computer thinking about how I'd not taken responsibility for anything.

What I had promised her was that I would live my life passionately and do all the things I really wanted to, not just for me but for her.

The day she told me about her condition she dropped it in like it was something she forgot to mention on a shopping list. Ki had got back from Thailand a couple of weeks earlier, and we had spent virtually every day together since. That day we were off to Brighton, and her dad was in the driveway cleaning his car.

'It's hot weather, na?' he asked.

'Good, isn't it?' I replied.

'Makes me want to go and visit some bitches.'

I looked at him as Ki came out. He continued, 'Na, beta, saying to Nina we must visit some bitches.'

'It's beaches, Dad, beaches. Yeah, we'll visit loads and we'll make sure we do it soon.'

I remember thinking that comment was strange as she normally took the piss out of his mispronunciations.

'Yours is into bitches, mine thinks I'm into porn,' I said walking back in with her.

'What?'

'I didn't realise that the Sky box downstairs was linked to the one upstairs, and I was flicking through it and lingered on a few porn channels and this lesbian talk show.'

She looked at me.

'It was just out of interest, didn't know I was interrupting Mum and Dad watching their Zee TV. Then in the morning I heard my dad tell my mum to talk to me, to have a word, maybe marriage would straighten that out. So she just left a couple more CVs on the table.'

'When will you tell them about Jean?'

'Soon,' I said.

'Tell them soon, Nina, it's not worth the wait. Do what makes you happy. You'll make sure you're happy, won't you?'

I looked at her. Where did that come from?

'I've got cancer, Nina, and it's bad. Phase three, that's what they called it. Don't think they can do much with chemo but they'll give it a go.'

She said it just like that, like she had bought some new trousers from French Connection and had forgotten to tell me.

She hadn't told her parents. Outside, her dad was blissfully ignorant; bucket in one hand, sponge in another, cleaning his shiny silver car and talking about bitches, unaware that shortly his life would change forever.

I deluded myself that chemo would sort it. I knew if I bargained hard and made a whole series of promises, it would be all right. Right until the last minute I believed that. Even when she died, I held on to her, not letting go. Her dad had to pull me off her.

The phone went again. 'Ms Williams is waiting for you in reception, Nina.'

'I heard you the first time,' I snapped.

My colleagues turned and looked at me. I never lost it. No matter what, I was always calm. Calm and reliable Nina, who worked twelve hours a day if necessary. Calm and dependable Nina, who did what was asked of her; who went to the gallery openings that nobody else in the firm wanted to go to.

I got up and went to reception to meet Boo. She was dressed in black and wore bright red boots, the colour of the dried tomatoes she had put into Venus de Milo's sockets.

'Sorry to have kept you waiting.'

'Quite,' she replied.

And that was it, the word that tipped me over the edge.

'Quite,' I mumbled.

'Yes, I've got better things to do with my time,' she replied.

'Like make apricot statues?'

Felicity looked up from behind the reception desk, shocked.

'I don't like your tone, Nina,' Boo said.

'I don't like your work, but there's nothing I can do about that, is there?'

'Nessun dorma', which was playing in reception, seemed to be playing unusually loud in my head as Boo started ranting. I wasn't really listening to what she was saying but just gazed blankly at her, watching her lips move and hearing the Guru's words telling me again and again that I was cursed. The only thought I had was to get out of there.

'Boo, Nina has been under the weather recently, haven't you, Nina?' Simon said, hearing her shouting and coming out of his office to try to placate her.

'Yes, under the weather, under a cloud, a dirty grey sky. I have to go, I have to leave.'

There was silence: the kind of silence that is desperate to be filled.

And Simon didn't stop me. Over three years at the firm, sweating blood, pampering over-inflated egos and making him money and he didn't even say, 'Come into my office, let's talk about it.'

Maybe if he had I would have stayed, because all that I needed was some reassurance that I was worth something.

'Right,' I said, getting my coat. 'I'll come back for the rest of my things later.'

'I'll make sure Felicity sends them on to you,' Simon replied.

I splashed through puddles, wandering aimlessly, feeling numb. I should have been elated, relieved at least that I had left work; but the way it had happened was out of my control, he was essentially showing me the door. After everything I had done, that's how much I meant. What would I say to my parents? Not only would I crush them by saying that I was marrying Jean but now my dad's biggest fear of me losing my job had come true. Perhaps it was better to break it to them all at once: if I didn't have a job I couldn't go through with their list system anyway so that didn't matter, and at least I had Jean. Jean would be there no matter what. He would return home later that evening and between us we could find a way to break it to them so that it wouldn't completely crush them. Things weren't that bad, I tried to convince myself. I'd just attempt to put the whole Guru thing behind me – there were good things to look forward to. Jean and I could finally settle down. I felt excited at the thought of seeing him again, having him wrap his arms around me and reassure me that everything would work out. As I had time on my hands I decided to go to his flat, make us dinner and wait for him: he was due back around six.

A short time later, my shopping basket was bulging with colourful vegetables. I had no idea what I was going to do with them but anything that had any colour went into the basket. Jean liked chicken so I decided to throw one in and figure out how to cook it later. I picked up a recipe book, some wine, flowers and candles and made my way to his apartment.

I smiled at the concierge as I entered the building, but instead of smiling back he glanced down at his feet.

'Busy morning, John?'

'Yes, miss,' he replied, calling for the lift. I could sense that he wasn't in the mood for chatting so I waited in silence for the lift to come down.

The tiles and mirrors reflected the huge ceilings of the apartment block and the lift was rickety and had an old-style caged door. I had always thought I'd get stuck in it. Before Jean Michel went away on his trip he had stopped the lift as we were halfway down. I had panicked. 'I'll take care of you, chérie,' he said. 'Always, you know I will. Nina, I want you to marry me.'

And although I was overwhelmed the first word that came out of my mouth wasn't 'Yes' but 'Dad'. All I could see was my dad's face, so absolutely crushed.

Jean tried not to appear disappointed. I asked for time to think about it. He said he understood, but now my head was clear I would have a chance to make it up to him.

We had met two years earlier at a party. The moment he walked in half the women in the room turned to look: he was six foot two, with blue eyes, jet-black hair and a big smile. I watched his every move from the corner of my eye and my heart jumped with disbelief as he made his way towards me.

'Are you OK?' he said in a deep, confident voice, as if he had always known me.

I turned to check that it was me he was talking to and that I wasn't mistaken: out of all the women in the room, he had chosen to speak to me.

We talked for hours and as I left he said he'd call. The days seemed interminable as I waited and my stomach did all sorts of things each time the phone rang. He called two days later, said he had wanted to phone straightaway to see if I got home safely but had held out as long as he could. There was something very solid about him: he was confident yet also excitingly passionate and spontaneous. There was no routine in our lives, no planning; things just happened.

He whisked me away from the world of the semi, Croydon and list systems, away from practicality and duty, and made me feel beautiful. He had all the qualities I lacked and when I was around him I never felt inadequate. Ki said he was what I needed; that he made me see things differently, beyond the values and concepts that had been drummed into me.

She, like Jean, was also a risk-taker, but ended up with someone who seemed safe, reliable and predictable . . . although he didn't turn out to be in the end. Ki was laid out in her coffin in her red bridal sari. Her boyfriend, who was supposedly madly in love with her, hadn't wanted to marry her, but her mother insisted that that was the way that she wanted to be dressed. Had she known towards the end that her boyfriend's visits had become more and more infrequent? He didn't even manage to make it to the funeral and three months later he was seeing someone else.

Jean Michel saw me through that period. Although my way of coping was just to get on with life and try not to think about things too deeply, I knew if I needed to talk he would listen. He always listened; he always tried to understand.

I turned the key to Jean's flat and it wasn't double locked.

'Careless as usual,' I thought. 'Goes away for four days and forgets to double-lock the door.'

I carried the shopping into the kitchen and thought

I heard a noise. Maybe the cleaner was in, although it wasn't her usual day.

'Hello,' I shouted. Nobody responded so I began unpacking the shopping. The fridge had half a bottle of champagne in it along with some pâté. There was another noise.

'Hello, is anyone in?' I said, going towards Jean's room.

Jean suddenly came out, making me jump.

'Jean, I didn't know you were home. When did you get in? Didn't you hear me? I've got so much to tell you.'

He looked very pale.

'Are you ill? What's wrong?'

His bedroom door clicked closed.

'What's going on? Who's in there? Who is it, Jean?'

'No one, Nina,' his voice sounded odd. 'Don't go in there.'

I went in and saw this woman emerging like some weasel out of a hole. She had a mass of red curls and was half-dressed.

All I could think about was the concierge, party to as many secrets as he was keys. He could have said something like, 'Miss, don't go up there, the gas men are seeing to a leak, come back in a few hours.' I would have listened.

I stood there, completely frozen, trying to comprehend an obvious situation. There were no clichés like, 'It's not what you think' or 'She's not important.' In a way I wish there had been because in those moments of silence I understood that he could not possibly love me and that he loved himself much more. He expected me to say something, to do something, but I just stood there in silence, staring at him. And then I walked away.

100 Shades of White

Preethi Nair

There's East. There's West. And there's Maya . . .

Maya, her mother Nalini, and her brother Satchin have left a carefree life in India to come to England. But when Maya's father disappears leaving only deceit and debt behind, they are left to fend for themselves in a strange, damp land.

Maya, though, doesn't know of her father's betrayal. Nalini, determined to preserve her children's pride, tells them that their father died in an accident and, as their struggle to make a life begins, whole realities are built on this lie. While Nalini cooks exotic pickles which enchant all who eat them, Maya begins to adapt to her new home – the unfamiliar food, the language, the music – and then to explore and make bold plans, plans that her mother does not understand.

But even a white lie cannot remain hidden forever – and when the truth resurfaces, it changes everything . . .

'Has all the ingredients in just the right quantities to spirit away all negative emotions.'   *Daily Express*

'Moving description packs a powerful punch in this book about family, forgiveness and the power of truth.'   *Guardian*

0 00 714346 X